Other books by John Scheck:

La Frontera Saga

Lines in the Sand

Twenty-Seven Calls

Lives of Crimes

Nothing Personal

CRIMINAL CODE by John Scheck

Published by LEFTBANKER PRESS

Library of Congress Cataloging-in-Publication Data

Author: John Scheck

Title: Criminal Code

Paperback ISBN: 979-8-9885351-7-1

EPIGRAPH AS PROLOGUE

After a truly remarkable life filled with intrigue and violence, the truly remarkable thing about the mercenary John Hawkwood (circa A.D. 1323 – March 17, 1394) was that he died in his bed, most likely of old age. A man who lived by the sword, and by all rights, should've died by it, too. But fate, or history in this case, has a twisted sense of humor and profound irony.

His name struck fear into the hearts of contemporaries and commanded reverence among chroniclers, blurring the lines between reality and myth. Shortly after Hawkwood's quiet demise, one legend was recorded by Franco Sacchetti—Florentine poet, part-time moralist, and gossip—who couldn't resist writing about the mercenary, at least now that this scourge was dead. In his 1399 collection *Il Trecentonovelle, Story 181* describes Hawkwood's mercenary ethic with a single, sharp exchange.

Two Franciscan friars visit *Giovanni Acuto*—the Italian name for John Hawkwood, also known as "John the Sharp"—at his castle near Cortona. They greet him piously.

"Monsignore, Dio vi dia pace" ("Lord, may God give you peace.").

Acuto swiftly replies with a bitter retort.

"Dio vi tolga la vostra elemosina" ("May God take away your alms.").

Puzzled, the friars ask for an explanation. Hawkwood tells them that, as a soldier of fortune, he lives by war; peace, to him, is as ruinous as the loss of alms would be to a friar.

It verges on blasphemy to propose a patron saint of mercenaries and assassins, but if such a figure were ever to exist, John Hawkwood, with bloodied sword in hand, would surely be first in line.

CHAPTER ONE

Spending any time behind the wheel of a car here would turn Gandhi into Charles Manson, he thought, speeding west on I-10 which at some point becomes the San Bernardino Freeway. He came this way on his first visit to Los Angeles years ago, knowing immediately he didn't want to stay and couldn't wait to leave. His low opinion of this city hadn't changed, considered by many to be paradise, the promised land, the place where dreams come true. If anyone were keeping score, he'd bet more dreams died here than anywhere on the planet.

What was it? It wasn't a city, not in any meaningful way. It was just an endless expanse of suburbs indistinguishable from each other, stitched together with mega-highways—some weighing in with eighteen lanes—and insane interchanges of five and six levels creating a driving environment more dangerous than any battle zone he'd ever known or even heard about. And forget about getting off the freeway and trying to go anywhere on back streets, which in LA could probably take days, or at least all day.

Most people drove as if they were in a race in which their lives depended on the outcome. He would've loved to stop someone and ask them where they were going in such a murderous hurry. What did they think they'd win at their imaginary finish line? What was the prize at the end of this asphalt rainbow? No wonder they shot at each other from their driver's seats, yet another act of barbarism rising precipitously in recent years. The big question was why didn't the people who had to deal with this toxic environment blow their own brains out en masse? How could they face this every single day?

Of course, there were no other transportation options open to him, considering what he had in the trunk. Even if he flew without this baggage, there was still the soulless commute from the airport to where he needed to be, somewhere called Torrance. From the satellite image of the area he studied during his planning, most of the man-made geography of LA was dedicated to the automobile. The city went all-in on the car while most European cities viewed the automobile as a huge mistake of the twentieth century that needed to be eliminated in the twenty-first or at least marginalized. For Los Angeles, there was no turning back.

He wasn't optimistic but assumed arriving in LA on a Sunday morning would be the best worst time to avoid traffic, if that made any sense. Now here he sat at a complete stop, bumper-to-bumper on a five-lane stretch of highway, ten lanes if you counted the opposite direction, also stopped for no apparent, visible reason.

He looked to his right and saw a guy about his age in an expensive European sports car. The joke's on you, he thought. All of that horsepower, leather seats, and state-of-the-art sound system and you're stuck here with all the others, slobs just like me in my piece-of-shit rental. Money can't buy everything.

He had another half-dozen exits, which at his current speed of stopped could mean he'd never get there, at least theoretically. He didn't want to go to Torrance, but he sure as hell didn't want to be stalled on the highway in LA, a level of hell Dante could never have imagined even in his worst, most feverish nightmares.

He started moving again. The sports car jerk-off switched lanes about four times before they came to another abrupt halt. They were side-by-side again, this time with the jerk-off to his left. Nicely done, moron. Where'd you learn that move? He could hear the jerk-off's sound system pounding out some godawful beats

5

that may have been appropriate at a drug-fueled disco at 3 a.m. Why is it the people with the shittiest tastes play their music at deafening levels? No one ever played Bach or Thelonious Monk at volume eleven in their cars.

He wouldn't even profane the music he listened to by playing it in a car, let alone on a freeway buried in a traffic jam. That would be like eating a gourmet meal while sitting inside a filthy dumpster. He considered getting out of his car, smashing out the jerk-off's passenger-side window with the barrel of his pistol, and asking him politely to turn the music down. It was just the boredom and frustration talking and he tried to return his attention to the audiobook on his rental's bare-bones sound system. Maybe he could turn up Hunter S. Thompson's *Hell's Angels* loud enough to drown out the dance beats.

His navigation system barked out that he had six exits before he needed to turn off, as if the voice were mocking his slow progress. He would've turned it off but there was no way he could manage without it. He wondered how anyone had lived in this superhighway apocalypse before these navigation tools became as ubiquitous as seat belts and airbags.

He almost missed his exit, which he imagined would have been an error on a par with the space shuttle being a few degrees off on its reentry trajectory into Earth's atmosphere. He still wasn't out of the woods as the San Diego Freeway southward was, without any doubt, the most nightmarish man-made environment he'd ever experienced. Exiting I-405 at South Western Avenue, Torrance spread out before him in all its charmless glory of industrial parks and commercial centers until he came to a halt at the law offices of Bishop and Sharp in a strip mall. It was the same lawyer he'd worked with before, but in remodeled digs.

Of course, it was in a strip mall, he thought. The law offices shared the shopping center with a trendy gym that was probably a different trendy gym a month earlier, a bakery, a chain restaurant, and a dozen other attempts at small-scale American entrepreneurialism.

Most of the businesses were closed this early on a Sunday and he had no trouble parking near the entrance of his destination.

Someone had evidently been waiting for him because the door to the offices opened just as he walked up.

"I'm Roland Bishop."

The last time, he met with the other partner. This one was tall, athletic, and about forty years old. He looked like a lawyer, even in his Sunday casual uniform of khaki shorts, leather moccasins, and a white shirt. He was surprised he hadn't introduced himself as Roland Bishop, Esquire.

Looking the part went a long way with lawyers, he thought. It went a long way in a lot of professions, but especially lawyers, at least the ones who went to court. Hollywood was exclusively about image and little else, so appearing like you were sent from central casting was even more important on this coast.

He'd done his homework on this firm and Roland Bishop. Married with two teenage children, Bishop graduated from a lesser state university law school, spent a couple years in the district attorney's office in some hick LA exoburb—probably because he had no other offers—then moved into private practice dealing mostly with personal injury, commonly referred to as an ambulance chaser and the bottom rung of the law profession, although not without its possibilities of financial reward for creative minds.

Not exactly a leading legal mind, this Roland Bishop, but anyone who knew anything about the profession understood being smart wasn't the only way to get ahead as a lawyer. Being ruthless and a willingness to cross ethical and legal lines was a sure way to financial gain. He already knew this was the path Bishop and his partner were on, or he would've never worked with them. The more prestigious firms had too much to lose dealing with the likes of the people in his profession.

The lawyer extended his hand.

"Mr. ...?" he paused, waiting for an answer.

He shook the lawyer's hand and walked past him into the office as if coming in out of the cold. He waited for Bishop to shut the door behind them before speaking. Conducting anything at all related to business in public was unnecessary. It was no longer paranoia when literally everyone in the world had a video camera in the palm of their hand.

"Just call me Tag," he said.

It was somewhat of an upscale strip mall, if there were such a thing, but the law office was the jewel and looked like a British country estate. Either the firm was doing very well, or they were trying awfully hard to look like they were.

Bishop led him back to his office where he offered his visitor a chair. Bishop was too arrogant to be nervous, he thought, but he's probably much more overconfident at other times when he's conducting normal affairs. Nothing like meeting a complete wild card like Tag to knock him down just a bit, at least at first.

"Mr. Tag…"

"Just Tag."

Bishop was taken aback by being cut off so abruptly, stammering a bit like he'd been tripped and had to recover his footing.

"Go on," Tag said.

"Yes. Ah," Bishop said, stalling out again as if lacking the speed to get his discourse off the ground. "Ah…we have a bit of a problem with one of our biggest clients, something completely outside of my purview."

Purview? Jesus Christ, how did lawyers ever get anything done with their ridiculous vocabulary? They think they're educated, but they're really just like people in the building trades or cops with a limited jargon they think makes them sound sophisticated. This thought put a grin on his face. Bishop obviously picked up on it, making him skip a beat in his pitch, or whatever he was doing.

"We're hoping you can, uh, fulfill the requirements…or ah, carry out our client's wishes in ah, a somewhat ah, in a very delicate matter. With, ah, complete discretion and, ah…"

Bishop obviously hadn't practiced his presentation and probably didn't know himself exactly what he was asking of this stranger except it was enough to get him disbarred and thrown in prison for a long stretch.

"As I said, this has to be treated with extreme care because of its…"

"Extra-legal aspect? Illegality? Criminality?" Tag said.

Tag had made his point but felt like rubbing it in, just to let Bishop know there was no need for prevarication.

"Felonious nature? Because of its possibility of landing us all in prison."

Bishop might not have been the sharpest knife in the legal drawer, but his face showed he understood.

"Yes, Mr. Bishop, I get it. That's why I go to absurd lengths to shield the nature of my services. That's why we've communicated thus far via encrypted messages from sources that would baffle anyone at the NSA instead of advertising on benches at bus stops."

It was a bit of a low blow, and he doubted Bishop and Sharp had bus stop ads, but they may have in their early years.

Bishop seemed about to apologize for even insinuating Tag needed to be reminded of the concept of discretion when he was cut off yet again.

"The only reason we're meeting face-to-face like this is I insist on it for these cases. For my own protection."

This rattled Bishop.

"What do you mean? How does it protect you?"

"You're the lawyer. You probably know why better than I could ever explain, Mr. Bishop. I need you to tell me exactly what you want me to do. If anything falls back on either of us, I need to have something along the lines of our mutually assured destruction. You can't sell me out to save your own skin if the shit ever hits the proverbial fan."

Bishop leaned forward, about to object, thought better of it, and sat back in his chair.

"Mutually assured destruction. Not a legal concept, but, yes, I understand your concern. My word against yours," Bishop said.

Bishop chewed on this for a bit.

"Not something I'd recommend as an attorney when counseling a client, although I suppose you have your reasons," Bishop said. "I get it."

Bishop probably assumed he'd come out ahead in that confrontation if it came down to it, Tag thought, so he voiced his position as he saw it.

"The word of a paid assassin against that of a scumbag lawyer? I'm OK with those odds. Please excuse the insult, Mr. Bishop, just making my point."

"Scumbag lawyer" wasn't an insult in Tag's opinion; it was a redundancy. And "assassin" was hardly his job title, at least not always.

"No offense taken," Bishop answered.

"Glad to hear it, Mr. Bishop," he said. "Since we understand each other, it's time to lay the cards on the table."

Bishop expressed himself even clumsier than before as he laid out what his client wanted, services Bishop and Sharp didn't advertise and offered to only the most exclusive and exhaustively vetted clients. Tag let Bishop do all the talking; he'd leave his questions for later, after he knew exactly what he was getting himself into, if he chose to accept. Few things would make him turn down the payday on this commission. It was all about risk versus reward and the reward on this was a risk in itself, he knew that. When the payday was this big, it could cloud his judgment about evaluating the risks. The reward this time was so high any consequences seemed insignificant. A dangerous perspective, and he knew it. Yet here he sat, listening.

These clandestine arrangements at Bishop and Sharp could have been filed under "Everything has a price," that is, if there were files kept, and, of course, there weren't. Just the tax evasion violations of the firm for these cash-only deals would have been sufficient to put the partners behind bars for half a decade.

Howard Sharp had been an accountant before going to law school, working for the Internal Revenue Service for four years before changing sides and specializing in tax law. The best tax lawyers hovered somewhere on the razor's edge of legality and as a former IRS gunslinger, Sharp knew precisely where to push and where to yield when it came to ensuring his clients paid as little in tribute to the state as was allowable by law. If this legal minimum didn't suit his clients, he could go further, for a price. He could've given a master class on money laundering, yet another of the blue-chip services available to a very select portion of the firm's clients.

The old adage that if you had to ask, you couldn't afford it certainly applied to these black operations of Bishop and Sharp, with the added caveat that if you asked for these services, you'd already committed a serious felony, like conspiring to be an accomplice in a capital crime. What was discussed on this particular Sunday morning in the strip mall office would've been more than enough for the California criminal justice system to put both men away for a decade, at least.

"Before we move forward, there's something you need to present to your client directly," Tag said. "And this may sound like fortune cookie bullshit, but it must be said."

Bishop didn't respond.

"Are you listening? This isn't negotiable. If I find out you didn't pass this on to your client…like because you don't want to lose your commission," Tag paused. "Let's just say you don't want me for an enemy."

"OK, of course," Bishop said. "What is it?"

"I'm not big on virtue, but turning the other cheek definitely points you away from ruin whether it's a bar fight or a Middle East war. Vengeance, whether by proxy or carried out personally, almost always turns to shit. It's a two-way street. Let her know that."

Tag wrote this last bit of criminal wisdom down on a sheet of paper and slid it across the desk to Bishop, ending it with an aphorism.

"Revenge had a price; consequences are extra," it said.

"What's this?" Bishop asked. "That Machiavelli or Sun Tzu?"

"I think I came up with that line. I have a lot of experience with getting even for whatever reason. What it means is that I'll be

13

successful with my assignment, but it won't end there. It never does."

Bishop didn't understand this either.

"She needs to hear this word-for-word. Got it?"

Bishop took the sheet of paper and nodded.

This aspect of the conspiracy lasted less than thirty minutes. The two men walked out of the law offices together and drove away in their separate vehicles: Bishop in his German luxury sport utility vehicle, and the clandestine operative in his nondescript economy car rented under the name of one of his aliases he used only for rental cars and hotels, using an Illinois driver's license and credit card. It always amazed Tag the things you could do with those two basic forms of identification.

The biggest risk about this commission, at least in the initial phases, was going to be driving around the greater LA area, he thought as he merged onto the San Diego Freeway northward on his way to Los Angeles proper, whatever that meant as it was impossible to distinguish one municipality from the next in this megalopolis of something on the order of 18.7 million people, all of whom seemed to be on the road on this late Sunday morning.

As he crawled toward his destination, he thought about one of his self-imposed rules he'd followed for most of his adult life. This little bromide was an attempt at humor he'd passed on to friends and anyone else who listened back in his days as a backpacker roaming around the globe, back before he'd even considered his current occupation, back before he'd considered any occupation at all. If you're traveling with more baggage than will allow you to outrun the average policeman, you need to shed some ballast. The lighter you are, the higher and faster you can fly.

He thought of this because he was wearing a belt around his waist with a few thousand dollars in cash, three state-issued driver's licenses with corresponding credit cards, and two passports: one American and the other from Spain. He had a few things in the trunk that would be impossible to explain if he were pulled over and searched, an eventuality he'd never allow under any circumstances, even if he had to resort to homicide, which was why he had a small-caliber semiautomatic pistol tucked away in the waist belt.

Getting pulled over doing the speed limit and following the rules of the road seemed almost impossible for a white male, but you always had to prepare for the worst. He always prepared for the worst, and then some—only a fool wouldn't. A simple traffic stop wouldn't escalate immediately into the Alamo. His Illinois license was bulletproof and would survive the deepest scrutiny, but if, for whatever reason—not that cops needed a good reason— he was facing an arrest, he'd do whatever it took to avoid that unacceptable outcome.

He'd done time at a state correctional institution in Pennsylvania on a breaking-and-entering charge—his one and only arrest. He didn't call his arrest bad luck just like it was stupid to call it good luck when he'd fleeced over fifty-eight residences in the hamlet of Gladwyne outside of Philadelphia, one of the richest zip codes in the nation.

Before his B&E career, he'd done a three-year apprenticeship for that occupation by working as a technician for a home security company. He never entered any of the homes where he'd worked, that seemed like an obvious common-sense decision on his part as

15

there were plenty of fish in the Gladwyne Sea with most of the older mansions clinging to alarm systems that could be shut off with the flip of a power switch. In the end, they busted him while he was driving home, giving him one more reason to despise cars. Over two years in lock-up because he was stuck in his vehicle—a mistake he swore he'd never repeat.

He also vowed he'd never return to prison, no matter what the price. If it came down to facing another stretch and a cop on patrol, even two, he'd already made up his mind how that would go.

He met few people who did what he did these days, at least some of the things he did. He liked working alone but he met a guy in New York he worked with on a job that a team. Some Wall Street asshole needed a good beat down, but the offended party didn't have the balls to do it himself and farmed it out—typical white privilege move. Tag and this one-time partner sat in a car for three nights waiting for the right moment and had a lot of time to talk.

Johnny was a fucking riot, Tag thought. A Brooklyn boy and mafioso wannabe except that lifestyle was fading into the sunset and existed mostly in movies and the memories of Johnny's uncles and grandfathers. Still, the kid was a fountain of stories of the streets, of petty crimes and grand thefts, of minor scrapes over bullshit, to shootouts with Black gangs.

But Johnny had a code, or at least he said he did.

"I'd never kill a woman or a child," he stated more than once in their stakeouts of the Wall Street asshole's haunts.

"Even with a huge payday?" Tag asked his new buddy.

"Couldn't be big enough. I gotta sleep at night, and no payday is big enough to get through those nightmares."

Tag doubted the generals running the show in Iraq during his brief career in the U.S. Army had trouble sleeping, and they'd killed scores of women and children. They'd launch a missile at a target with less thought than most folks would put into choosing a movie to watch that evening. There was no amount of "collateral damage" his superiors considered a problem, yet Tag was dishonorably discharged for a single unsanctioned killing. He was lucky with the dishonorable as the U.S. Army tribunal had considered a stint in a military prison.

A human life was a human life. There were no age or gender requirements. What difference did it make? He'd never killed a woman or a child—at least not directly or knowingly because in Iraq he'd been in firefights too desperate to keep score. He'd witnessed first-hand the aftermath of a Hellfire missile attack that killed an entire family of nine, including two infants. He couldn't count the civilian carnage left behind in the wake of artillery assaults on villages. The civilian death toll in the Iraq War was impossible to calculate with anything remotely approaching accuracy. Tens of thousands? Hundreds of thousands? A million? No one knew and no one who mattered cared.

No one cared about the Iraqi Tag shot dead after his squad was ambushed on a dirt road one night, not really. Three of Tag's team members died in the blast from an IED, and three others were injured. The survivors spread out to make a perimeter. Tag came upon a kid kneeling in a ditch off the road trying to detonate another explosive device, belted him in the head with the butt of his rifle, cuffed him behind the back with a zip-tie, and frog-marched him back to the vehicles.

The Humvee carrying the wounded and KIA sped away just as another convoy of three vehicles came to a halt. A lieutenant colonel hopped out and saw Tag holding the prisoner on his toes by pulling his cuffed hands up high on his back. The Iraqi's face was bleeding from the strike from the rifle butt and his overall appearance was grim, although not all of it the fault of this American corporal who'd captured him. The prisoner was filthy, with wild hair and a ratty beard.

"Take your hands off him, soldier," the lieutenant colonel screamed.

Tag, as always, did as he was told.

"Any mistreatment of prisoners in this battalion will not be tolerated," the crusading light colonel said, as if addressing his own ego and place in history as he saw himself.

Just from his ordered appearance and pressed fatigues, Tag could see he was probably some admin REMF (rear echelon mother fucker) just passing through from one heavily guarded base to the next.

"I'll take charge of the prisoner."

With that, the officer cut the prisoner's flexicuffs and was about to hand the Iraqi a bottle of water when the bedraggled kid turned around and punched the officer in the face then tore away at a full sprint. The officer squealed in pain and bent over with both hands covering his face.

Tag raised his carbine and instinctively shot the Iraqi teenager between the shoulders when he was sixty meters away.

A single shot at a moving target at night. The kid was probably dead before he hit the sand. Tag's teammates who'd survived the earlier carnage were awestruck by the shot. The lieutenant colonel realized he'd received nothing more than a slap from the Iraqi. Embarrassed by his mishandling of the prisoner, he took out his anger on the corporal who'd just seen five of his squad members torn apart from a blast set by the dead insurgent.

And so began the young soldier's slow and inexorable march out of the United States Army. Tag had nothing in the way of a defense against the charges, except he knew if the officer hadn't cut the kid's cuffs, he'd still be alive. The Army was trying to make up for a lot of lost ground as far as human rights violations in their invasion. As in the Abu Ghraib prison scandal, a low-ranking soldier would receive the full and righteous fury of the American military justice system.

Civilian life for Iraq War veterans was difficult for most, and even more so for those unlucky enough to have left with a less than honorable discharge. Tag saw generals on TV talk shows who'd probably been responsible for the killing of thousands of civilians, war heroes who'd go on to run for office, attach their names to ghost-written books, or continue upward in the military hierarchy. Tag came home and felt lucky to find a minimum wage job installing alarm systems.

Tag never had the luxury of developing a moral code, especially not while in combat in Iraq. He had teammates who'd been shot at by women and children often enough to assume everyone and anyone was a potential combatant, but he'd never put his sight on a woman or child and pulled the trigger. He was absolutely sure he wouldn't have hesitated a split second had the situation called for him to kill anyone who posed a danger to him or anyone in his platoon—his only code.

Tag respected the sanctity of women and children simply because they'd never got in his way. He'd never taken a job to kill either of these two supposedly forbidden demographics, but there'd never been an offer. That's about as far as he'd thought about the issue. He based his acceptance of a job on the price and the risk and not much more. There was no room in his deliberations to split hairs when it came to gender or age or morality. The mere thought of this seemed absurd to him, considering his line of work and the things he was paid to do. Thinking about what he wouldn't do for the right price was a parlor game he'd never bothered to play. It was either worth the risk or it wasn't, nothing more.

***

He'd heard of Beverly Hills, of course, he'd even been there briefly, but he had no idea there were a staggering number of levels of class and status within this ridiculously expensive area of Los Angeles. Imagine owning a mansion in Beverly Hills and feeling you lived on the wrong side of the tracks, he thought. The French had the right idea during their Reign of Terror back in 1793. If America were still capable of anything in the manufacturing arena, they should start building guillotines for the next revolution.

He didn't feel the least bit self-conscious or inferior as he drove up into the hills in his basic sedan, but he felt this vehicle stood out from every single other vehicle on the road, a point he'd consider when he picked up a new rental. Then he thought the servants of these modern-day royals probably commuted to their masters' estates in this class of automobile. Once this idea came to him, he noticed the people in the modest cars seemed to be the only drivers following the rules of the road. Many of them were undocumented immigrants with almost as much to lose as he in the case of a traffic stop.

This gave him his first idea on how to proceed, his Trojan Horse into the confines of the rich and powerful.

CHAPTER TWO

The property once belonged to a heavy metal rock guitarist who sold it for sixteen million dollars to the current owners, it was worth a lot more, but the market was weak, which isn't ever the correct word for the Beverly Hills housing market. Of course, before the new tenants condescended to set foot on the two-acre estate, the entire interior was gutted and remodeled by the most celebrated interior designer of that week. The complete renovation was the class equivalent of an extermination, a purge of the previous residents and everything they represented. The new residents were the exact opposite of rock and rolling all night and partying every day, or the opposite of that (partying all night, rocking during the day, which seemed slightly more appropriate). The youngish power couple were considered part of the changing of the guard from old Hollywood to the streaming future of movies.

Walter Greene had a very typical ascension into the lofty realm of movie production which meant he had almost no interest in film until he saw the money through the trees. Harvard undergraduate and then a Wharton MBA, lured to Hollywood from Wall Street after the writing was already on the wall about the future of the film industry. The changing movie world was like an orchard ready for the harvest.

Just as music had gone from vinyl, to cassette, to compact disc, to digital, the movie industry evolved as quickly and radically over the course of two decades. From the ubiquitous VHS video rental shops in every strip mall in the country, to the modernized version of DVD which stood for digital versatile disc—something no one knew during the product's brief lifetime, and why bother learning that bit of arcana after its demise? Those technologies went the way of the dinosaurs, leaving consumers with collections of music and movies on platforms no longer supported.

The entertainment industries never offered to reimburse consumers if they wanted to upgrade their considerable investment in media to the newer technology, while they fought tooth and nail to prevent piracy of their precious intellectual property. Secondhand shops were soon filled with the detritus of the usurped technologies, then landfills became the final resting place of the planned obsolescence. All those who'd never bothered to learn how to program a VCR felt vindicated, but everyone felt they'd been swindled by the progress.

Walter Greene made his initial fortune during the tech bubble in the early 2000s. He'd been assigned by his Wall Street brokerage firm to assess the climate in Seattle in 2002 when initial public offerings (IPO) were just beginning to make unbelievable fortunes for the select few in the inner circles of rising software companies. At first, it was only the truly innovative and ground-breaking entrepreneurs who were turning their visions into vast fortunes. Getting in on the ground floor of these companies was for a select few: the top engineers, and the businesspeople who built the companies from scratch.

As company after company shot to stratospheric heights when they chose to go public, a pack of jackals smelled the scent. Almost overnight dozens of companies popped up in Seattle, dot-com medicine shows and snake oil salesmen offering everything and anything. There was nothing new to their collective sales pitches except this time it was all over the new marketplace: the internet.

It was an insane moment in the history of capitalism, and one of its lowest. A handful of very clever people who'd never made anything anyone ever wanted to buy discovered a way to fleece anyone who'd ever believed investing in the stock market was an honest way to make a buck. Walter Greene didn't even need to be in his First Avenue Seattle office to understand what was happening.

He'd be sipping a martini after work in one of his favorite bars in the Belltown neighborhood when the place would be invaded by a group of twenty-something kids who were on a sponsored field trip. They'd come into the bar and literally drink the place dry as a supervisor would put down his platinum card to cover the entire tsunami of overindulgence. Without anyone asking, all the liquored-up kids could talk about was their dot-com miracle company and how many employees worked there.

"We have two hundred and twenty employees!"

Walter Greene had a tough time trying to get any of these overly-enthusiastic new employees to explain exactly what their company did. He doubted any of them had any idea of the true goals of their employers. The Wall Street financial analyst had an exceptionally good idea of what was happening.

What happened was one of the biggest transfers of wealth in the history of humanity, mostly from the middle class to the new elite, the hyper-rich. There were dozens of dot-com companies that never had anything in mind except a plan to fleece investors while making huge fortunes for the few clever swindlers who made up the core of these internet enterprises boasting they'd revolutionize the way Americans bought dog food, or plane tickets, or how they placed advertisements online.

Companies that a couple of months earlier were boasting how they had office chairs for their employees costing small fortunes, in-office masseuses, and dozens of other shameless excesses, now had stock prices at pennies a share while all of the initial investors had already sold out after the first day of trading, walking away with everything.

Walter Greene made a staggering fortune on this game of three card monte. It was too easy for someone with his training and experience not to come out far ahead on the ridiculous speculation that exploded in the stock market spurred by the swindlers in Seattle.

With his enormous fortune made, Walter Greene was ready to move on to the next chapter of his career, his next mountain to climb. Hollywood.

Walter Greene had married his college girlfriend while he was finishing his program at Wharton. He was twenty-four and his bride was twenty-two. Two children seemed to arrive before Walter even knew what was happening as he was spending eighty hours a week at his office in Manhattan while he and his wife tried to maintain a family and a home in Connecticut.

His wife was only the third woman he'd ever slept with in his life, something that pleased his wife but the more he thought about it, the more it haunted him. He saw men his age and many much older, men he worked with who were single and had their pick of New York's most beautiful women. Of course, he loved his wife and his children, but why had he been in such a hurry to take that course? He'd never even taken a vacation as a single man, not once.

There was a broker in his group who'd been at Wharton when he was there, although they barely spoke back then. They both landed at the same firm in New York and got to know each other as they trained together during their first few months. Gustavo was from Spain. Barcelona, Walter thought. They were both extremely competitive, you had to be in their chosen field. From the very beginning, Walter slowly edged ahead of the rest of the new recruits and after three years, Gustavo worked under him.

That should have been enough for Walter. He'd won, he was on a direct path to the top, and while Gustavo had a bright future with the firm, he'd never rise as high as Walter was destined to soar. There wasn't a single investment analyst in the entire firm in Walter's league. He was a star, and everyone knew it, yet Gustavo bugged the living shit out of Walter.

On the rare occasions when Walter had a drink with people from work, Gustavo was always there with a woman, a different woman almost every time, and they were all stunning. Over the course of two years, Walter had seen Gustavo with six different women, and they always were on very intimate terms, these weren't just friends. Gustavo was imperiously tall and had just the slightest bit of a Spanish accent to make him sound aristocratic while making monolingual slobs like Walter feel inadequate, and of course, Gustavo also spoke French, not to mention Catalan.

In the early 2000s, the CEO of the firm hosted a party at his penthouse for the top employees to ring in the new year. A new tuxedo for Walter (his first), a designer gown for his bride of eight years now, a sitter for their two children, and the Greenes were excited to be at one of New York's most exclusive gatherings, the kind others would read about in the morning newspapers.

No one would ever accuse Walter and his wife, Sharon, of being madly in love, but they got along tolerably well. Both were overwhelmed with life: Walter with work and Sharon with the two children and the house. Walter truly didn't give his marriage and family life a lot of deep thought. It's just something men did. It's what his father did.

Most of his friends were in the same situation—not that he had time for friends. He'd never considered cheating on his wife. Christ, how would he find the time, he thought.

He took a good look at his wife as they soared to the penthouse in one of the building's six high-speed elevators. Sharon looks good, he thought. She was never a real beauty or hot, but she was an attractive woman. It's not like Walter was any prize as far as his looks, but he knew that didn't matter much for men. What counted for men was status, money, and power and he was gaining more of these commodities with every quarterly statement of his section at the firm. He was on his way to achieving everything he'd ever dreamed of and even more.

And then he saw Gustavo at one of the five bars set up in the penthouse for the party. Gustavo looked like a Spanish movie star or a professional polo player, a presence which he managed to pull off every day. Even at the end of a grueling fifteen-hour day at the office, Gustavo looked like he'd just showered and changed clothes. He greeted Sharon with all the charm of a television game show host. It didn't bother Walter in the least that Sharon could barely control herself around the Spaniard. Who could blame her?

"Allow me to introduce my dear friend, Astrid. Astrid, this is Walter and his lovely wife Sharon."

Astrid. She was almost as tall as Gustavo and Swedish, or Finnish, or from one of those countries that manufacture circus-freak gorgeous women. Blond hair, cobalt-blue eyes, and she spoke flawless English, of course. She was beyond perfect, Walter thought, and worst of all, he knew she and Gustavo were screwing.

Walter didn't know it a minute before meeting her, but he knew he didn't want a Sharon. He wanted an Astrid.

Two years later when Walter moved to Seattle for his firm, he went alone, leaving Sharon with the house in Connecticut, the two children, and a generous divorce settlement to assuage the tremendous guilt he left behind. This time around, Walter planned to live without any regrets and not make the same mistakes. After six months in Seattle in which he mostly lived at his office, he started to date a waitress at one of the bars on First Avenue. She moved in with him less than two weeks later.

Walter didn't know it, but he was a serial monogamist and couldn't live without a girlfriend in his life. It was impossible to discern what part this new woman played in his life as their sex life was unremarkable and infrequent, she was an even worse housekeeper than Walter, and they had absolutely nothing in common. He'd replaced Sharon with another Sharon. A little over a year later, she dumped him.

His job kept him too busy to care much about his personal life as he was now making more than anyone at his firm except the top officers. He also helped to engineer the takeover of a small internet video company from Seattle that was on the verge of moving into the booming internet streaming world pioneered by a former DVD rental company. You don't always have to be first or even any sort of an innovator to make it in a business like the entertainment industry. Even a guy with Walter's education would find it impossible to calculate what Americans were spending on entertainment every year. All Walter wanted was a small piece of an extraordinarily big pie.

With Walter's migration to Hollywood, he promised himself he'd be up to his eyebrows in Astrids. That was part of the compensation package for the major players in the film industry along with making vast fortunes. He'd been in Los Angeles for less than three years before he married an actor who'd had a modest career in television. She was no Astrid, not by any means, but she was no Sharon. Two years later, they had a daughter. Life wasn't much different at home for Walter than in his Sharon days except now he wasn't wealthy, he was fabulously rich. As far as Walter Greene could tell, he wasn't happier, but he knew he'd rather be successful than happy.

Success for Walter Greene meant following in the footsteps of another company that transformed what everyone thought was a dead-in-the-water online movie rental company into one of the largest producers of television content the industry had even known. The idea was so revolutionary you didn't need to be first to hit paydirt. A string of copycat companies hitched their wagons to the same idea of producing content for the rapidly expanding TV online platforms.

Walter's contribution to the ascendency of the dot-com miracle had nothing to do with the creative end of the company. He'd been responsible for a spectacular capitalization that allowed the company to produce an almost infinite string of movies and serialized TV programs at the precise moment when the internet was capable of providing these services to any household in the nation with a cable online service.

If the idea had been pitched two years earlier, the technology wouldn't have supported the dream, a few years later and the competition would have proven insurmountable. The company's achievement wasn't simply about being at the right place at the right moment in history, but timing played a crucial role.

Walter Greene was richer than he'd ever been, and he'd been a rich man for a long time, but anyone with money will admit, once you achieve a certain degree of financial security—and it's a fairly modest level—an extra zero or two on your bottom line doesn't translate into added well-being, whatever the hell that was. What was happiness? For Walter, he'd had moments of it pass through his life, like rising up a grade on a rollercoaster. He could remember certain events in his life he thought had brought him happiness, or something like it. They weren't all victories in the business world. The births of his children had been joyous, but if he were being completely honest, four or five of his biggest one-day windfalls as a broker had been more of a high. He wasn't proud of this and wouldn't have admitted it to any living soul, but he couldn't control how he felt.

He met his new wife when his company was just getting off the ground before they were even beginning to produce their own content for TV and films. Walter was visiting the set of a TV police series he was looking to acquire for his company's struggling online series department. Barbara Wilson (née Tristan Orwell from Fremont, Ohio) was one of the stars of the program which was doing moderately well in the extremely competitive market. Divorced, no kids, and currently involved with a middle-tier method actor who was more talented at substance abuse than anything the public had seen of him on film.

He had one of those trendy-sounding names that was probably generated by a tool in a word-processing program. Tattoos, just the right amount of facial hair to make him look like he'd slept in his car for three days, and a belligerent demeanor that had landed him in jail on three occasions. Barbara couldn't wait to move on when Walter showed up on the set representing the exact opposite of Johnny Dangerous, or whatever his name was.

Barbara simply ghosted Johnny Dangerous, Mr. Rebel Without a Career and moved in with Walter three months later. Not that he cared anything about Barbara, but the ex-boyfriend felt it necessary for his tough-guy image to make a few threats in Walter's general direction as well as insulting Barbara around other people in the industry. He'd never said anything to Walter's face because a minor actor and a major up-and-comer Hollywood producer inhabited separate chambers in the palace, but Walter heard about the threats and insults second hand.

Walter had never been in a fight in his entire life, not even as a child. The mere thought of it terrified him, so there was no question of Walter confronting the actor. So, like cowards and powerful men throughout history, he had someone else do his fighting for him. In this case, Walter sent two of his office assistants to deliver a letter to the loudmouth has-been, and soon to be out-of-work actor. One to deliver the letter, and the other to film it in case the actor tried to shoot, or punch, or slap the messenger.

The two assistants were just out of university and thrilled to be working so quickly in the industry, even though they were both on the bottom rung. Neither of them had ever heard of the actor to whom they were serving papers, or a paper. It was only an envelope with initials on it, and from the weight there couldn't have been more than a single page inside.

"Any idea what this is about?" assistant one asked.

"None. And why do we need to film it?" assistant two asked.

"Must be a legal thing, like serving a subpoena."

They weren't told anything about the nature of the letter or the recipient, and certainly nothing about the love triangle between their boss, his current girlfriend, and the obscure actor as Walter would have imagined they wouldn't have accepted the assignment, even if it meant dismissal. Physical courage was a scarce commodity in the movie industry, both for those in front of the camera and behind it.

Walter's two Ivy League thugs, who together couldn't have physically intimidated a cub scout, pulled up in front of the modest Malibu bungalow and practically skipped up to the door, wearing nearly identical business suits neither could afford at this point in their nascent careers, but they were on that first important rung on the way upward and knew looking good meant everything in the business. One held the letter, the other brandished his digital camera like a weapon, ready to capture the moment.

This was back when only the most progressive companies were a fraction as politically correct as everyone was expected to be ten or fifteen years in the future. The two assistants were sometimes referred to as the Twin Twinks, as many people in the office assumed they were lovers. They weren't, at least not yet, and even they didn't take offense to the nickname no one used to cause offense—the two of them were too highly regarded for anyone to insult or allow them to be insulted. They were new, but everyone who knew anything realized they were going places.

They were held in high esteem and destined to rise quickly because neither of them ever took a bit of shit from anyone, ever. While they looked like a pair of groomed Yorkshires, when push came to telling someone to fuck off and die, they were pit bulls, plain and simple. If Walter told them he didn't have time to talk to anyone that morning, no one got through to Walter. Queen of

England, Elton John, Magnum PI, didn't matter who you were claiming to be on the phone, you weren't getting through to the boss. Not on this morning.

Twink with the envelope beat on the door like it was his hairdresser after a botched dye job. Twink with the camera was a few steps back like he was ready to begin his entry in the latest film festival. Before the door opened, they could hear the bellowing inside, mostly indistinct ramblings with the occasional bit of profanity standing out clearly, like the only words of a language you understand.

The door opened.

"What in the living fuck are you doing at my door at this time of the morning?" the has-been screamed.

"Um, it's not even close to morning. Maybe in Japan."

It was two-thirty in the afternoon in LA, to be precise. In Tokyo it was six-thirty.

Has-been couldn't wrap his head around the math or the humor and fell back on profanity.

"The fuck do you want?"

Twink with the envelope held out the summons.

"The fuck is this?" Has-been asked, even more belligerent, but now considering the many ill omens the letter could bring.

Court summons? Childcare delinquency notice? Bank overdraft? Foreclosure? He had a lot of demons looming over his life, but he continued to play the tough guy role with the two queers at his door.

"Get the fuck outta here, faggot."

Randall Perkins hadn't been called this in his entire twenty-three years. It almost made him laugh. He didn't laugh. He pushed the letter into the chest of the homo-hater.

"Get that the fuck outta my face."

Randall was as calm as if he were talking on the phone with his mother.

"As charming as this conversation has been up to this point, you need to know this comes from Walter Greene, the CEO of Overlord Productions, or chief executive officer, in case you're too clueless to know that acronym. Do you know what an acronym is?"

"Fuck you…" Has-been shouted.

"Just take the letter mister…whoever the fuck you are. That's how little Walter thinks of you, he didn't even bother to give us your name."

With that, Randall put the letter in the drunk's hand and walked away, walked away into the legends of Overlord Productions. There was no celluloid gangster tough-guy who surpassed Randall Perkins' scene filmed by his coworker that day at the Malibu bungalow.

After he'd seen the Twin Twinks' video, Walter imagined the actor read the letter and crawled back into his dark hole of drug and alcohol abuse while anything approaching a career in the industry slipped further out of his reach. The letter was a few sentences explaining what would happen to the actor if he so much as mentioned the names of Walter Greene or Barbara Wilson ever again. The letter was signed by Walter as well as the heads of two of the city's biggest studios.

Walter felt powerful, and power made him horny, or at least it made him feel he could have his way with women, or a woman. Sexual desire was constant in healthy males, for other men less blessed in this area, these needs came and went like an occasional craving for some obscure dish. If Walter's current girlfriend—and future wife—kept track of their sexual relations, it would have been a disappointment for most women, but she had different goals.

Barbara Wilson didn't sleep with Walter Greene to get a part in a film. She already had a job when they met, but it's not like she was immune to his status in the city. Walter was already wealthier and more powerful than all but the very top tier actors, a few of them TV actors in Barbara's circle. After her fling with the asshole, Barbara welcomed the stability and boredom of a studio executive with thinning hair and a body that seemed resistant to the demands of his personal trainers.

Barbara hadn't worked since her series concluded just after she and Walter were married. They felt this would be a suitable time to start a family and a year later Emily Greene was born. After having a daughter with Walter, Barbara worked even harder to keep her body in movie-star shape. She wanted to work again but wanted to reenter acting with just the right role. She was married to the right guy to make this happen.

The life of a top Hollywood movie mogul is filled with even more temptation than any fiction created about this world. Even a former putz like Walter Greene who never dated in high school, and only began in his senior year at Harvard, even a guy who looked like a high school driver's education teacher could find himself with women literally throwing themselves at him. All it took was being the CEO of one of the companies revolutionizing the film industry.

The first time Walter cheated on his new wife was the third month of her pregnancy. He'd just finished a meeting with the producers and director of a new TV series that had started shooting. One of the producers figured it couldn't hurt to have the head of the company completely behind their project. He'd sized Walter up correctly as sexually frustrated and awkward as hell when it came to women. He brought along four actresses to the meeting whom he'd coached beforehand.

"One of you has to take one for the team, or two, or all four if Walter is a greedy bastard. It'll mean a lot for the show, and it could also be incredibly good for your careers."

After the meeting, the producer brought the four actors into Walter's office.

"We need an extra for the series, a small part but recurring. Very few lines. It's mostly about the right look. I think you should make the decision, Walter," the producer said, and he left Walter alone with the four hopeful candidates. "We'll respect your opinion. If you think more than one of them are qualified, we can work them into the script."

Walter chose only one. The other three left immediately, leaving Walter alone with his choice. His first affair took place on the sofa of his producer's Hollywood office. More than the act itself, Walter was most impressed with how easy it'd been. They hadn't talked on the phone, didn't go on a couple of dates, no conversations where he had to impress. She'd simply closed the door to his office and walked toward him as she undressed. He didn't say a word to her until after.

Of course, it was easy. It was an act of prostitution, an underhand softball pitched to Walter by the TV producer. Walter didn't put two and two together and thought it was simply his vast charm and charisma that led to the young actor losing control.

As soon as he reached orgasm, Walter was overcome with guilt for cheating on his wife. Before he broke down completely, the young actor got dressed, kissed him, told him what a wonderful time she had, and left. He didn't know her name and for days agonized whether or not he should contact her. Send her flowers? Money? What was he expected to do?

If you were looking to have your way with women, being a major Hollywood player was a very good way to go. Walter's dalliances came less from sexual urges than a desire to compensate for the times other kids made fun of him because he was a total social outcast in high school and unable and unwilling to defend himself, something that haunted him ever since those days. Any guidance counselor or psychologist could have told the boy everyone feels awkward and alone in high school; you have to constantly remind yourself things improve in the next stage of your life.

Walter should've spent his time in therapy instead of grudge-fucking women who just wanted a chance to be in the movies. None of his liaisons were the least bit healthy or based on mutual attraction, relying on the unequal power balance between the parties. The more he took advantage of his position, the less he cared about the women involved, to the point where not only was he unconcerned whether they enjoyed it, the fact that the sex was mostly nonconsensual was an added turn on. Walter became a serial lecher, but as increasingly creepy and criminal as his encounters became, he felt he was helping the women with their careers. This was little consolation to most of the victims who felt powerless to complain, and there was no *quid pro quo* in Walter's charmless sexual advances.

The public side of Walter Greene was that of a devoted husband, one half of a Hollywood power couple. Barbara had taken on a new role in a TV series that was in its second season and doing moderately well, thanks to the zealous promotion from Overlord Productions.

The couple's purchase of the former rock star's mansion was big news for a week, or at least a weekend. Although the estate had been a big financial move for the couple, Walter's career had since made a stratospheric leap between the time they closed on the property and when the renovations were completed ten months later. One of Walter's strengths as a film executive was that he knew people would watch what they were told to watch with little concern for quality.

"I think we need a bigger house," Walter told his wife before they'd even moved in, not even aware of the line he was paraphrasing came from a blockbuster film starring a man-eating fish.

The truth was Walter wasn't a fan of movies. He didn't read, didn't play sports, didn't play a musical instrument, and had no hobbies. He'd spent his entire adult life either studying business or working as a businessman. He'd never been to Europe, didn't have a passport. He hated vacations but indulged his wife with trips to Hawaii where he spent most of his time on the phone out of the sun. He thought the beach was the adult equivalent of playing in the mud; he was a poor swimmer, so the ocean in Hawaii scared the living shit out of him.

Barbara stuck to her guns on staying at the rock star mansion as she'd overseen all of the reconstruction, although she knew nothing of interior design, architecture, fashion, or modern art. What she did know was a home had to reflect something of the people who lived there. There was little in the current state of the manor that reflected the new inhabitants, but of the former rocker residents, there was no trace, and all it took was two million dollars in renovations.

Walter Greene's ego shrank with every story in the local press of someone building a new mega-mansion with a heliport and a price tag four or five times more than what he'd paid. His wife asked him how much house they needed, when was enough enough? All Walter knew was if someone else had a more expensive property, it meant they were winning. Worse than not winning was losing and he'd come to hate losing. Funny for a man who despised sports as a kid.

CHAPTER THREE

Dive bars were one of Tag's great passions, and he was a student of the genre. This place was about as far from Beverly Hills in character as possible, but it was the nearest place where people who worked in that wealthy district could afford to live and drink. He sat at the bar chugging a Mexican beer that was unremarkable but popular in the USA. After slowly nursing two beers, he saw his prey enter the bar, or at least he was fairly certain it was the guy he was after. He'd seen him stop here the day before at the same time.

He was alone, which worked out well for Tag as he'd be easier to approach. He sat two stools down the bar. It was just after five in the afternoon, and the place was empty except for these two at the bar and a couple playing pool.

The target ordered a beer.

"Put it on my tab," Tag told the bartender in English, then he turned to the target, "*Me tocó la lotería ayer. ¡Cinco mil pavos!*"

Tag knew enough about human nature to know if you wanted to get a working man talking, just mention the lottery.

"Thanks," the target said in Spanish. "Congratulations."

And then, after giving it a bit of thought and taking a deep drink from his free bottle of beer, he continued.

"Where're you from?" he asked, continuing in Spanish.

Tag gave away that he wasn't Mexican by the slang he used for "bucks," which is "turkeys" in Spain.

"Madrid."

"Nice," was all the target could muster for an answer.

"I wasn't born there, but that's where I learned Spanish," Tag said, by this time giving away he spoke Spanish with an accent that, while reflecting the patterns spoken in Madrid, also revealed he was a non-native speaker.

Tag had spoken Italian as a child at home in the USA and spoke Spanish with a slight Italian lilt.

"Ha, in Mexico, we still think of the Spanish as gringos."

"Yeah, I got that a lot when I traveled in Mexico," Tag said.

"You been there?"

"A few places," Tag answered.

"You like it?"

"Some places."

"What's the best place you visited there?"

"Guadalajara," Tag answered immediately.

"No shit, that's where I'm from."

Tag already knew this, and he'd never been to Guadalajara before, but he took a crash course on the city the night before in case he had to answer any questions. After three days of tailing this guy, he knew his name, the house he shared with three other men, that he was born in Guadalajara, had been living in California for the past three years illegally, and probably didn't have a valid driver's license in California.

He figured this last part out the second he followed Alberto Mejía in his fifteen-year-old economy car. Either he was driving without a license, or he was a driving instructor. They needed to make everyone drive like they were illegal aliens, Tag thought, because the legal people, especially in LA, mostly drove like complete assholes.

The other things Tag learned about Alberto Mejía he gleaned from looking through his mail while everyone in the shared house was away at work.

For the price of a beer and a compliment about his hometown, Tag was on his way. He bought another round, then another before he steered the conversation to what he was after. He didn't ask Alberto any direct questions about where he worked, but began by telling him what he did.

"I install alarms for all the strawberries," Tag said, this time using the Mexican slang for posh people. "It doesn't pay much but I don't have a green card."

"My job is OK. I'm a gardener at the Greene place. You know it?" Alberto asked.

"No. Is it nice?"

"Used to be some rock star's place a couple years ago. Yeah, it's pretty sweet and the pay is better than most guys like me make."

Tag didn't want to push things. After spending three days to get this far, he didn't want to blow it by making the guy suspicious, a common state for illegals who feared a lot of things normal people never had to consider.

"Listen, Alberto, I gotta go. Maybe I'll see you again. You live around here?" Tag asked, already knowing the answer.

"Yeah, just a couple blocks away. I can walk if I get too drunk."

"I'll be back in this area on Thursday. Maybe I'll see you then," Tag said.

Alberto wasn't there on Thursday, but Friday he was right on time. He and Tag started up right where they'd left off before. Alberto had never met a gringo who spoke Spanish before even though Los Angeles was about fifty percent Hispanic. His English was pretty basic even after living in the USA on and off for almost ten years. It was hard learning another language, especially when everyone you knew spoke Spanish. At his job on the estate, he never needed to speak English as the housekeeper who managed all of the service workers was Mexican.

"So, the guy at the gate," Tag said, holding up one finger.

"The security, yeah."

"Two gardeners, and you also take care of the pool," Tag said, holding up two more fingers.

"They got another guy comes once a week or so just to check the chemicals."

"Then there's the maid who helps the main housekeeper," Tag said, now with four fingers in the air.

43

"And their chef," Alberto said.

"No way! They got six full-time people wiping their asses for them? I guess that's how rich people do it. Asshole's probably never pumped his own gas," Tag said.

"From what the house cleaner tells me, he don't even flush," Alberto said with a howl of laughter.

"*¡Qué cerdo!*" Tag said.

What a pig, indeed.

Tag's idea to curb the excesses of the hyper-rich would be to make them do all of their own housework and maintenance. Go ahead and buy a forty-room mansion on four acres, but you have to cut your own grass and clean your house. The thought of some rich slob pushing a mower through chest-high weeds, or a yacht rotting to pieces from neglect made him laugh. But that wasn't going to happen any time soon. The new elite were infinitely more privileged and out of touch with the people than the French aristocracy at the time of their revolution.

For his own part, Tag refused to hire part-time help to clean his two residences. Even the obsequious nature of restaurant workers made him uncomfortable and the fact they relied on tips for their living was repugnant to him. Servants, servitude, servility, subservient, and other words all stem from the Latin for slave.

The U.S. military had a built-in class system with its division between the enlisted and officer corps. Tag never saw the value in it and thought it was more outdated than any other institution known to mankind. Most traditions from our past had either been abandoned or had evolved to reflect a more enlightened society, but religion and the military had resisted change over the centuries. Their evils, their dark secrets, and their ineffective ways had remained hidden as both organizations were too powerful to be changed from the outside, and no one inside would admit to any internal problems. The military was even more rigid in its ways than the church. There had never been an equivalent to Martin Luther in any of the world's armies. "Military reform" was the soundest, most bulletproof oxymoron Tag could imagine.

He'd been drummed out of the service by an officer who'd never been in a firefight in his twenty-year career. Tag had fired his weapon in combat too many times to remember. He shot a fleeing prisoner, a prisoner who'd most likely been responsible for the deaths of three of Tag's teammates in an IED explosion. Just like they do in civilian criminal court cases in plea bargains, the prosecution had threatened Tag with a considerable prison term if he didn't agree to the terms of his punishment. This meant if he fought and lost against what he thought was a ridiculous charge of killing a man in a war zone, he'd spend years in a military prison, a worse sort of hell than combat, from what he'd heard. He faced the same no-win proposal when he was arrested on the breaking and entering charge: accept the plea deal, or go to trial and if he lost, he'd face maximum sentencing guidelines. It wasn't the old carrot and stick routine; it was the stick and the bigger stick.

Just like his public defender on the B&E charge, his JAG lawyer was less than useless and criminally incompetent. In both of his judicial hearings, he felt he could've done a better job defending himself. Both of his appointed attorneys had simply allowed themselves to be brow-beaten by the prosecution and had agreed to everything presented to them. He vowed to never go through that process again, no matter what.

No matter what. That was an incredibly broad statement, impossible to define, too vague to even warrant a definition, but Tag had spent quite a lot of time pondering what it meant to him. In order to avoid another run-in with the horribly flawed justice system, he was definitely willing to run from the cops if they tried to pull him over. If he were detained somehow and couldn't talk his way out of it, then, well, he'd get away, no matter what.

By any means necessary.

If that meant killing a cop, he'd do it. He'd already made up his mind. He knew that's how it had to be because there'd be no time to make that decision on the spot. Just another part of the code, he thought.

***

Six full-time workers represented just a part of the staff at the manor of Walter Greene. Twice a month, a cleaning crew came into the house to wash windows and thoroughly scrub the bathrooms and kitchen, just to give the full-time people a leg up on the enormous task of maintaining the sprawling residence. Someone came at least once a week to take care of the home's five saltwater aquariums. Whenever the couple hosted a dinner party, extra staff were brought in for serving and cooking. They often hired string trios or quartets to play at events both indoors and in the pool area.

In addition, a piano teacher came once a week to try to coax their fifteen-year-old daughter to play. Walter and Barbara had separate personal trainers who came to the house two or three times a week, time permitting. If Walter couldn't make time at home for his sessions, the trainer came to his downtown office. The total bill for the maintenance on the home, the fish, and the residents came to over half a million a year. It was difficult even for a whiz-kid graduate of the Wharton School of the University of Pennsylvania to precisely calculate the intricacies of his benefits package, but Walter managed to include absolutely everything he could in tax exemptions. He was doing very well by any standard. Money was not a problem for Walter Greene.

According to recent studies on human happiness, there is a point where money has no further influence on a person's well-being. Walter Greene earned four hundred times this benchmark income associated with a life free of financial worries. How happy would Walter be if he raised four hundred other people up to the exalted level of not having any money concerns? And forget about how many suffering souls he could have raised out of abject poverty, but men of his ilk were driven by forces few people could understand, motives driven solely by ego and dark, competitive urges.

Only six years after moving into the mansion once owned by the campy band leader, Walter felt his initial buying price of sixteen million dollars and the multi-million-dollar renovation somehow came up short of what he was worth at this juncture in his ascendancy to the summit of the Hollywood hierarchy. 2,000 square meters? There was a new super-mansion being built that would be three times that size. Once again, Walter felt he'd settled for a Sharon and not an Astrid.

The couple stayed put because Barbara loved the place, and why wouldn't she? It was a sprawling estate with a tennis court, swimming pool, seven bedrooms, and a parking area accommodating twenty vehicles. What was there not to like? But Walter was concerned about his image and his spot in the pecking order of the Hollywood aristocracy. He'd recently heard one lesser

Beverly Hills mansion described sarcastically on a Hollywood insider website as a glorified mobile home.

The weakest aspect of the home, in Walter's estimation, was that it only had seven bedrooms. Every time he heard that mentioned about his manor, it made him wince. The fact he, his wife, and their daughter used exactly two bedrooms made no difference in the math used by anyone keeping score in LA, and everyone was keeping score. He actually proposed to Barbara that they split two of the guest bedrooms in half, thus upping their total to nine bedrooms, but his wife was considerably less driven by whatever demons of status that tortured Walter and rejected the idea.

When he and Barbara purchased the estate, they paid several million less than everyone knew it was worth because of the worldwide financial crisis, and even at that discount, Walter had to leverage everything he had at the time to push the deal through. That was years ago, and at his current compensation, he joked that now he could put this house on his credit card instead of the elaborate schedule of payments he designed when he purchased it from the rocker.

Walter's insecurities robbed him of any joy and sense of pride he should have gained from the home. All he could think about was moving out and moving upward just as soon as he could talk his wife into it. Barbara said she'd consider it after their daughter turned eighteen in three years. Walter wasn't sure if he could take three more years of slumming.

CHAPTER FOUR

"'This is how the industry works,' were his exact words. That's what he said right after he'd forced himself on me," the actor said to the lawyer recording the deposition.

Pilar Domingo had made the quintessential meteoric rise in the film industry, capturing the leading role in the film adaptation of the blockbuster hard-boiled police novel, *Twenty-Seven Calls,* in which she played a Philadelphia police officer secretly targeted by a real estate mogul whom she'd seriously injured during a domestic violence call at his concubine's apartment.

"Ms. Domingo, we'll need more specifics of the crime. 'He forced himself on me' isn't a legal concept," the lawyer said. "And while this makes for an arresting opening, we'll need to begin at the beginning."

The lawyer kept the video rolling as the young actor pushed back from the desk into her chair.

"Let's see. The beginning would be when my agent called me to say I had a follow-up for the audition I did for the series pilot of *Thanks for the Memories.*"

"My wife's favorite series, by the way," the lawyer interrupted. "I don't get a chance to watch much TV I'm afraid."

Lawyers, Pilar thought. She'd rarely met one who read or had any interest in movies, even those who worked in the industry like this guy, but she wasn't here for a conversation about her filmography and started her testimony all over again, back several years ago.

She began.

"Pilar," Pilar's agent said on the phone.

"Rudy, please tell me you have good news. I'm putting groceries on my credit card as we speak," Pilar said as she pushed the cart with one hand and held her phone with the other.

"You got a callback for the reading you did two weeks ago, for the series," Rudy said.

Rudy Greenberg wasn't exactly what anyone would call a high-powered agent, but he had a few extremely successful clients who stayed with him after they struck Hollywood gold, grateful he'd signed them as nobodies.

"You aren't a charity case for me, Pilar," he'd told her when he'd signed the actress. "I don't do *pro bono* work. I believe in my clients, every one of them."

This was comforting to Pilar at that moment in her life when she was waitressing and auditioning for every local theater part, film extra role, and feminine hygiene commercial she could ferret out in the LA acting scene. Dominican by birth, she'd grown up in Queens, raised by a single mother with three children. Her father died in a traffic accident when she was in high school but had enough bearing on her life to guide her toward an arts degree from the SUNY Empire, Manhattan campus (The State University of New York).

"So, what did they say?" Pilar asked, referring to the callback.

"You know how they are. They didn't say shit, just that you need to be on the lot on Thursday at ten o'clock. They'll make you wait around all damn day," Rudy said. "You know the drill. Slightly better than a cattle call."

Pilar had been making the rounds long enough to know she needed to manage her expectations. She was called back four times on a small TV part and wasn't offered so much as a role as an extra without lines. Still, would it kill or cost these people anything to give out a compliment or two? A little more than the stock, "We're going with another actor," would do her ego a world of good.

She borrowed a roommate's car (she shared a house with five others, four of them actors) because she was terrified her piece-of-shit would break down on the forty-five-minute drive and she'd miss the audition, or maybe it was just another reading. She arrived at the lot security gate an hour and a half before the appointment and was told she couldn't enter until forty-five minutes before her scheduled time. Even at this early hour, it was warm in Burbank.

Great, I'll just sit in the car and melt for forty-five minutes and then look like hell for my audition, she thought.

She returned to the security gate precisely forty-five minutes before her appointment. Between parking and finding the office, she walked in ten minutes before she was scheduled, which for her very un-Latin sensibilities, was late. She'd barely sat down in the cramped waiting area with the five other candidates when an impossibly beautiful blond woman opened a door.

"Pilar Domingo?"

"That's me."

The blond stunner gave her a bored look and waved her through the door.

Pilar truly would have welcomed sitting around for an hour, maybe a few hours, so she could collect herself, and she had nowhere else to be. Instead, she was still sweating from the hike from the parking lot and overwhelmed with anxiety over an audition that could change her career as she made her way down a long corridor and then into some sort of conference room with a table big enough to seat a Thanksgiving dinner for the entire Kennedy clan.

Typical Hollywood overkill, she thought. There were four people at the table: a guy she recognized as a director on the rise; a woman in a business suit that probably cost more than Pilar's used Subaru, who she assumed was the casting director, based on her other run-ins with this breed of Hollywood player; another woman in hippie clothes, who could be a writer or simply the cleaning woman they were using to stack their deck; and an executive type in his late fifties, if she had to guess. She thought he looked like one of the maintenance crew in a very expensive designer suit.

Her father had been a notorious *refranero*, difficult to translate into English but the term referred to someone well-versed in Spanish proverbs. Her father could match a Spanish proverb to literally any situation in life and he did this, at least at times, to the utter exasperation of his family.

Upon seeing the well-dressed maintenance man who, of course, wasn't a laborer, one of her father's sayings sprang forward almost instinctively: "*Aunque la mona se vista de seda, mona se queda.*" Put a monkey in an Armani suit, and he's still a monkey.

"This is Pilar Domingo for the part of Andrea Moreno. Pilar, this is Rafa Ortega, the director, Marsha Davenport, the writer adapting the story for the series, and Tanya Mills, our casting director," the stunning blond said without mentioning the over-dressed man at the table.

He sat in silence leering at her. There was no other way to describe it, and Pilar felt she had an excellent vocabulary. She was asked to read again while the casting director filmed. Then she was directed to sit across the table from the four people who would decide her fate. The suit didn't say a word.

Pilar and Rafa conversed amiably in Spanish. She learned he was Mexican-American and had lived in LA his entire life. The casting director told Pilar she was one of three actors they were now considering for the role, down from six candidates before the meeting. The writer-hippie asked her a series of questions about her upbringing, which Pilar thought were entirely superfluous, but she answered as guilelessly as she could manage.

Only when the meeting appeared to be over did the casting director introduce the suit.

"This is Walter Greene, the CEO of Overlord Productions. He wants to have a few words with you before we make our decision," Tanya Mills said. "Thank you, and we all hope we can work together."

A few handshakes and kisses on the cheek from Rafa, and Pilar was now alone in the conference room with Walter Greene, who hadn't said a single word during the preceding twenty minutes. Why would the head of the studio be here at the audition for a not-very-important part in a new series? This became abundantly clear almost immediately.

Walter stood up from his chair at the conference table, and still without saying a word, he held Pilar by the shoulder, undid his belt, unzipped his pants, pulled out his erect penis, and sat down on the corner of the table. Had Pilar not been completely ambushed by this behavior, she would've acted differently, but she was flabbergasted, even more than intimidated. When Walter began masturbating and groping her breasts, the young actor was overwhelmed with fear, embarrassment, shame, and the helplessness of servitude.

She wasn't willing to become a prostitute to get a part in a TV series, or for anything else, but she couldn't bring herself to move, to speak, or to resist. It was like she was watching the scene from outside herself. She did manage to take a step away from his hand on her breast. The movie executive climaxed with a whimper, then took a tissue from his pocket and cleaned himself. The horror had lasted less than a minute, perhaps less than thirty seconds, although for Pilar it was an unimaginable eternity.

Walter pulled up his pants, tucked in his tailor-made shirt, zipped up, and buckled his belt. He still hadn't spoken a single word.

What a fucking charmer, the dumbfounded actor thought.

"This is how the industry works," Walter Greene said, and without waiting to hear a response, he walked out of the conference room.

Even before Pilar could register the horror of what had just happened, she could only think about what an incredibly ugly penis the mogul sported. Small, of course, surrounded by a ridiculous mound of pubic hair, but the most hideous thing about his organ was that it looked as if it'd been cut off and sewn back on. Pilar had enough experience with men to have seen a few penises that were somewhat lacking in aesthetic appeal to the point of repugnancy while others were beautiful. Without a doubt, Walter Greene had the ugliest cock she'd ever seen.

Pilar sat back in silence to signal to the lawyer she'd finished.

"And you had no further contact with Walter Greene after this incident?" the lawyer asked.

"No. Incident? Is that what it was? I've been wondering all this time, which is one reason why I didn't go to the police afterwards. What would I have told them? That he jerked off on me? More like jerked off near me or in my immediate proximity."

Pilar took a moment to sit back and collect herself.

The lawyer held a piece of paper in his hands.

"You got the role and you never saw Greene again?"

"I got the part. I suppose Greene was just giving me his stamp of approval, or whatever. I've seen him a couple of times since then, but always around a lot of people. I saw him in a restaurant a few months ago with his wife and daughter, I assume. I wanted to walk up and tell them all what an ugly dick he has and how I came to see it."

"Did you ever mention the incident to the director?" the lawyer asked, checking his notes. "Rafa Ortega."

"No. I don't think he was complicit, but I had no way of knowing. I just wanted to work," Pilar said. "I didn't mention it to anyone, at least not until I heard stories about him from other women."

55

"Do you remember the first woman to accuse Greene?"

"Kate Barlow, the actress. This was back on the third season of the series. She was nineteen or twenty. She had a small part in the second episode, but she nailed it, so they wrote her into the remaining episodes.

"It was a small cast, so we knew each other, at least a little. She called me in tears after a shoot one day and told me that ugly cock boy did the same thing to her. I went over to her apartment, close to where I was living in Manhattan Beach. She was trembling like a leaf. I remember feeling nothing more than fury over what that fucking pig did to me, but Kate was shattered."

"She didn't report it?" the lawyer asked.

"It was her first acting job, like the absolute very first, other than a couple bits in commercials, basically all she had on her reel. How was she going to report it without jeopardizing everything?"

"This seems like his *modus operandi*, preying on the weak and vulnerable," the lawyer said.

"Absolutely, at least the ones I've heard about. A makeup artist on the show told me he cornered her in her trailer, reached under her skirt, and shoved his fingers in her pussy while he masturbated," Pilar said. "Is that specific enough for you?"

The lawyer didn't respond.

"Three from a single series. Any others?" he asked.

"None I talked to, but who knows? I only got the story from the makeup artist because I came in not long after it happened and she was still crying. She didn't want to say anything, of course. Too humiliated."

Pilar was getting angry.

"That's the worst part: he made these women feel ashamed. That's just so sick and twisted and it makes me want to smash his head with a hammer."

Pilar Domingo had spoken with several other women who'd been sexually assaulted by Greene, but none of them wanted to press charges.

"They all either have too much to lose, or like in my case, how badly could I hurt him even if he were put on trial?"

"Your case would pose considerable problems for the D.A."

"I know. Like why didn't I say something six years ago when it happened? After that, it's simply his word against mine. No evidence, no stained dress, no witnesses. Hell, I didn't even tell anyone until Kate spoke to me, like people swapping stories after a shared disaster."

"I'd like to get statements from all of the victims. Do you think they'd agree to that?"

"Some, maybe, but as I said, most have too much to lose by coming forward. I'll ask."

Pilar had nothing else to say and stood up.

"More than anything, I want this asshole to stop doing this. I hate the fact he's getting away with his creepiness while the women he's left in his wake of perversity are suffering."

Pilar stopped before reaching the door of the office.

"Maybe I could write him an anonymous letter warning him he's being watched."

"That's really not something as a lawyer I can help you with or even encourage."

What the fuck good are you then, Pilar thought.

"I hope you can understand I'm bound by my profession and anything outside of the law is, well, not something in my wheelhouse," he said.

"I get it, thanks."

Pilar was about to open the door.

"With that said, I know some other people you may want to talk to, at another law firm. Let's just say they aren't as bound by the tenets of their chosen profession."

He had her full attention now.

"They're down in Torrance. Officially, I have nothing to do with their firm, but I can put you in touch with a third party who can set this up if you want."

Pilar wasn't sure at all what he was even proposing. It sounded dark and sinister. She'd had her own dark and sinister ideas whenever she thought about Walter Greene.

The law firm on Wilshire Boulevard in Beverly Hills dealt mostly in A-list celebrities and was considered one of the leaders in entertainment law. If you wanted an airtight contract with a movie studio, or the best possible compensation package for your film, prize fight, record deal, or football season, then Strauss, Merkle, & Randolf was the place to go. In addition, they had very qualified attorneys for criminal defense and civil matters.

She'd been represented by another Beverly Hills powerhouse when negotiations began for the role she landed for the police drama, *Twenty-Seven Calls*. Her firm drew up the contract and even subtracting their usual percentage, it was more money than she'd earned in her entire life up until this point. Like many actors, she wasn't interested and didn't care about money matters, not that she had anything against making money or being rich, but she'd grown up in a poor family and continued to live on beans and rice, in spite of her stratospheric income.

Another actor who'd be her costar in the new film told her about his law firm and said she should give Strauss, Merkle, & Randolf a call. Before she signed the contract for *Twenty-Seven Calls*, she scheduled an appointment at the firm.

What attracted her to the office was the fact the first person she dealt with, a kid barely out of Stanford Law, had read the book the film was based on and knew her entire filmography.

"This movie is going to be a fucking monster, are you kidding?"

The kid was practically foaming at the mouth with enthusiasm. She spoke English with Danny Madrigal as he was something of a lapsed Mexican-American who could defend himself in the language of his parents, but, as he explained to Pilar, he was much less of a lawyer in Spanish than English.

"Your deal with Johnson & Talbot is an insult," he said. "Can I ask you a personal question, Miss Domingo?"

A personal question? In a law office about a contract? Why not, Pilar thought.

"Sure, shoot."

"Can you play a total badass cop?" the kid asked. "Honestly, I don't even need you to answer because I know you're going to totally fucking kill the role of Beth Owens. I swear, when I read the book, from the very beginning I saw you in the role."

"Don't bullshit me, Danny," Pilar said.

"No shit. The scene at the apartment, when the rich asshole punches her in the face, then tries to grab her and she launches him off the ground and slams his head into the doorway...that's you," he said. "Am I right?"

He was right, Pilar thought. She'd thought the same thing when she read the novel and had focused on that particularly iconic scene.

The deal promised by Johnson & Talbot was good, but conservative. The kid wanted to roll the dice. Of course, he didn't have that authority and could only send his recommendations upstairs to one of the partners. They were able to cut a deal for points on the sales of the film, something almost unheard of for an actor who, although successful and on the rise, was far from a proven box office draw.

Strauss, Merkle, & Randolf signed her for less than Johnson & Talbot had guaranteed, but with a percentage of the sales, charging their cut only on what she'd later earn on the points. This meant the firm would make nothing until the film reached an agreed upon sales figure at which point Pilar Domingo would be paid three percent of the gross, with Strauss, Merkle, & Randolf taking their cut from this.

It turned out very well for Pilar and her new representation. In spite of the film's poor marketing strategy—at least in the opinion of Pilar's newest and biggest fan, Danny Madrigal—*Twenty-Seven Calls* beat out a superhero movie at the ticket counter on its release, establishing Pilar Domingo not only as a star, but a legitimate box office draw.

She could now pick and choose her parts and to follow up the hard-boiled crime drama, she helped produce a time traveler fantasy from a book by the same author of *Twenty-Seven Calls*. Strauss, Merkle, & Randolf walked her through a similar deal with the new contract. The studio agreed to pay less in salary while giving away another point of the sales, as if they were betting against the success of their own film.

"I can't even believe they're going for this, but you should absolutely take it. You stand to make ten times more," Danny said before the papers were signed.

As Pilar was part of the production aspect of the film, she solicited the opinion of her young lawyer on matters of the film's marketing.

Danny Madrigal wasn't simply a casual fan of movies; he'd been studying the industry since his undergraduate days in economics at Princeton. Had he not been drawn to entertainment law, he would've worked as a statistician at the World Bank. He was a numbers guy in the world of lawyers that valued words, but he knew movies and he read voraciously.

"Numbers and science don't lie," he was fond of saying whenever it was appropriate.

For his Ivy League undergraduate dissertation, Danny conducted an extensive analysis of book sales and how they related to the success of the film adaptations. His biggest frustration for the dissertation was the shoddy sales statistics he often had to weed through on his way toward uncovering the truth. Quite often, especially in the not-too-distant past, there wasn't much concerning the demographics of sales figures. Danny was not some gypsy fortune teller, but whenever he had proper numbers dealing with the age of book buyers, he was able to extrapolate from these numbers a very solid prediction on how the film version would fare in theaters.

He was also an insatiable reader and had a sense for which novels would translate well onto the screen.

"If there are no scenes in the book, if you can't recall a single episode, it just won't work on film. The movie will never get off the ground. Pigs can't fly."

There was an old adage in Hollywood that good books make bad movies, and the opposite is often true. Danny disagreed with this completely. Bad books never made good movies. Period. If the movie did well, there were elements in the novel that were remarkable. Period.
The book for Pilar's newest project, *Autobiography of a Time Traveler*, was full of iconic scenes in Danny's estimation. He was on to something because the adaptation of the novel went on

to be the third biggest grossing film of the year with a budget of less than a quarter of the two comic book films that beat it out.

CHAPTER FIVE

Strauss, Merkle, & Randolf was much more than a boutique law firm catering to a few elite clients. At last count, they employed a team of thirty-eight lawyers, with the majority of them specializing in contract law, while at least a half-dozen members were top authorities on property rights as they dealt not only with the residential real estate ventures of their celebrity clients, but also any incursions they made in investment properties. Tax law was another major concern among their customers, and this department had its own floor of the firm's four-story building on Wilshire Boulevard.

A big part of the legal work done at Strauss, Merkle, & Randolf was trying to keep their clients above the law and out of trouble, but as anyone who's ever read a newspaper or watched the evening news knows, once in a great while, Hollywood stars get arrested. For these unfortunates, the firm had three criminal defense attorneys on call. The last time a client of Strauss, Merkle, & Randolf was charged with a felony, all three defense lawyers worked on the case. Not only that, but the firm considered the charges to be serious enough and the consequences potentially so detrimental for the client it was an "all hands on deck" situation for all employees. Every lawyer and admin person in the house was expected to be up to speed on the case and investigating options for a defense.

There was a simple philosophy at the firm which was to maximize earnings for clients in their contracts, ensure they paid as little in taxes as allowable by law, keep their business dealings on the up and up, and then come to the rescue if any client got caught up in the American criminal justice system, for whatever reason.

With one hundred percent of their business model dealing with keeping everyone and everything legal and above board, it wasn't ironic that clients often came to them when they had problems that needed extralegal solutions. Who better to plan a crime than people trained to keep criminals out of jail?

If a client broached a subject involving any sort of illegal activity, it was like the firm went into a quarantine drill. The client was immediately handed over to the firm's top investigator, an ex-Los Angeles police detective who also happened to have a law degree from Loyola Law School in LA. The firm would've never considered hiring anyone with a degree from LLS for their legal staff, but this investigator with a law degree had proved to be exceptionally useful on many occasions, and the truth was Marty Evans knew about as much about the law for his narrow purview as anyone at the firm.

The ex-cop was called on when a client needed to be directed to someone outside the firm who was both capable and willing to step outside the law for a price. For anyone but the top clients at the firm, they would've been told that Strauss, Merkle, & Randolf was a law firm and not the mafia. The hyper-rich usually get what they want, at least if they're willing to pay for it. While Strauss, Merkle, & Randolf never got involved in these matters, they acted as brokers. They wanted happy clients.

Marty Evans' first task was to vet the clients. In the initial phase, he tried to talk them out of the path they were on which quite often could put them behind bars, even if they were only making plans. He looked exactly like who he was: a tough ex-cop who'd seen it all and maybe twice before on the streets. His job was to let clients know what kind of world they were entering if they chose to continue down this path.

After twenty years as an LA cop, Marty had come across every sort of shitbag, hustler, gangbanger, hired assassin, pimp, and thug-for-hire the city produced. This was the world these rich assholes would be entering if he couldn't talk them out of their plans. Clients from the firm looking for dark solutions had a wide variety of problems including stalkers who couldn't be dissuaded by restraining orders, ex-lovers who threatened to write tell-all memoirs, honey pot traps where sex tapes were made and huge sums demanded to keep them private, extortion schemes, and sometimes murder for hire requests.

Once the investigator knew clients were determined to go ahead with their plans with or without the help of the firm, he directed them to the next stage which was putting them in contact with the right people for the job. He wasn't allowed to broker directly with these dark web sources as this would have tied the Beverly Hills law firm directly to criminal activity. Marty Evans facilitated contact between Strauss, Merkle, & Randolf clients and these agents of darkness, usually by burner phones. The firm relied on Marty's discretion forged from his long career battling the underworld to ensure nothing could get back on them.

Another of Marty's responsibilities was to guarantee these outside firms didn't hustle the clients in any way. This wasn't to say they couldn't charge the clients whatever they wanted for the services they provided, but any dissatisfaction on the part of the Beverly Hills clients would merit a follow-up investigation from Marty Evans, something Marty didn't particularly enjoy, and something the outside firms desperately tried to avoid. There wasn't much in the way of an upside in pissing off Marty Evans.

For what Pilar had proposed, Marty felt the best option was to call on the small law firm of Bishop and Sharp in Torrance,

California. While the offices of Bishop and Sharp were only twenty-five kilometers from the elite Beverly Hills law firm, it was in a completely different world, at least in some of their negotiations. Marty knew that while they were a legitimate law firm, their real talents were in money laundering, at least that was how they began building their catalogue of illegal services. Once you enter into the world of making money for desperate criminals, you make a lot of contacts among people who have very unusual skill sets.

Marty suggested clients send someone in their stead when they met with the Torrance people and any clarifications on what they were looking for could be sorted out with messaging between the client and their proxy. The Torrance people insisted on meeting people for these discussions at their office. Although this never went over well with the Beverly Hills clients who weren't too keen on venturing into the wilds of Torrance, a place for them as foreign as any fly-over state.

Marty couldn't talk Pilar Domingo out of her crusade, out of her mission, out of her desire for justice, for revenge, her promise to the victims to hold Walter Greene accountable for his crimes. She also insisted on meeting with the Torrance people herself.

Marty was mesmerized not only by her beauty, but by the way she carried herself: imperious, confident, yet possessing a certain humility he'd never encountered in the hyper-rich assholes he dealt with at Strauss, Merkle, & Randolf. What she wanted, what she was asking for? He would've done it himself had she asked.

Pilar Domingo had an ally in Marty Evans. It's good to have allies.

Very against the policy of his employers, Marty agreed to accompany Pilar on her meeting with the Torrance people. If they'd known, he would have been fired, but maybe not. He knew too many secrets at this point. Marty Evans had never married, had no children, was collecting a decent pension from LAPD, owned his home in Malibu he'd purchased twenty years ago, and had saved a sizable portion of his income since he began working as a cop at twenty. He had a level of financial freedom almost unknown among men his age. He liked his job but if he lost it, he wouldn't miss a beat.

Marty picked Pilar up at her Manhattan Beach townhouse, and they drove to Bishop and Sharp Law Offices in Torrance, pulling in at dusk, well after business hours. Before they got out of the car, Marty made one last appeal.

"Last chance, Pilar," Marty said. "You don't need to meet this guy and, as I said, I don't recommend it."

"I feel bad enough hiring someone to do my dirty work. I don't mind taking some responsibility, even if it's just looking this guy in the eye."

The door to the offices was locked but before Marty could ring the bell, it opened and Roland Bishop ushered them inside, locking the door again behind them. Marty guessed Roland had put on a fresh suit for the meeting with the movie star as Marty had before he went to her house.

"Roland, how're you doing?" Marty said. "Been a while."

"It has. Good to see you, Marty," Roland said like he really meant it.

"Roland Bishop, this is Pilar Domingo…" Marty began.

"Of course, I know who she is," Roland said. "I love your work, Ms. Domingo."

Pilar nodded.

That was it for the pleasantries and the three of them took seats in the conference room.

"This is a bit ridiculous, but I have to ask. Is Walter Greene a client of Strauss, Merkle, & Randolf?" Bishop asked.

Marty shook his head.

"Well, let me begin by pointing out that this man is, without getting too much into the operational jargon, a hard target. I have no idea what sort of security measures he has for his home, but it's also important you know he has a wife and child who will probably be there."

"To be honest, I don't give a fuck about his family, or collateral damage, or whatever it's called. This is all on him."

Marty was totally shocked by Pilar's outburst; alternating levels level of vitriol and sangfroid she left out of the hours of videotaped depositions she gave at the firm which he'd studied astutely.

Walter Greene sexually abused the wrong woman, Marty thought.

"I doubt he gave a moment's thought to how his actions were injuring other people."

Roland Bishop pushed out his jaw a bit as a sign that this seemed right to him, at least on some level.

"I'm not even a hundred percent sure this is even doable, but I got a guy in mind who I've worked with," Bishop said, then turned to Marty. "Your man, as a matter of fact."

"I was thinking the same thing," Marty said.

There wasn't much else to discuss.

"I'll set this in motion," Bishop said. "As far as a fee, I'll need this initial retainer in cash."

He wrote a figure on a small note pad and handed it to Marty who showed it to Pilar.

"Let's say three business days? Is that a problem?" Bishop asked.

Marty didn't think it would be, but he looked over at Pilar.

She nodded.

"Three days. I'll bring it here on Thursday morning," Marty said.

It was getting dark as Marty led Pilar out of the office. She wore dark glasses and a full headscarf, like an Iranian princess. She couldn't be too careful as Marty advised and there was nothing to be gained by someone recognizing Pilar Domingo walking out of a Torrance law practice.

"Who is this he was talking about?" Pilar asked once they were on the road.

"Ms. Domingo…"

Pilar hated when he called her that, but Marty insisted, she was a client after all.

"I really need you to understand something, something extremely important. I can't think of any situation in which the phrase 'the less you know the better' has greater significance than this one here, which I'd still like to talk you out of."

"Marty, not again. We've been over this."

"OK, but if I can't talk you out of it, you need to know this is something I can never discuss with you. You can't mention this to anyone ever again. And this isn't just about any possible legal ramifications. I'm talking about your own mental well-being, your ability to sleep at night."

"What makes you think I sleep at night? Do you think the women he's raped sleep through the fucking night without waking up from some horror they can't shrug off?"

Marty nodded at this, as if to say, "fair enough."

"Even so, trust me when I tell you that you don't want to know anything about this world. I don't want to come across as the hard-assed cop, the seen-it-all veteran of the streets, but I really am that guy, so believe me when I tell you this is a world you want nothing to do with."

Pilar said nothing.

"Take my word. You have nothing to gain and everything to lose by having any more involvement in this affair than you do already at this point."

They drove in silence for a few minutes until Marty pulled off Highway 1 and headed toward the beach.

"As much as I wish you'd give this up, I respect what you're doing. I told you I'd do it myself if I thought I could get away with it. It's out of your hands now, so you need to get it out of your head."

"Thanks, Marty."

Marty thought that was it.

"And I get it, Marty, but I'm not some rich twat who doesn't have any idea of how things work. I grew up very poor in New York City. To be perfectly honest, I've had dates that were more traumatic than what Walter Greene did to me, but this isn't about me. It's about all the other women, both in the past and in the future."

Marty turned onto The Strand.

"I don't know, maybe you think I'm some heartless cunt because of what I said back there about Greene's family, but if it took someone to harm his wife, or even his daughter for that fucker to stop raping women, I'd sign off on it."

"I don't think you're heartless. I admire the shit out of you for doing this, for taking this risk because you want to stand up for others. Maybe I'm in the wrong business—fuck, I know I'm in the wrong business. I don't get that feeling much doing what I do, almost never."

"What feeling?" Pilar asked.

"People, lawyers, clients, absolutely fucking anyone doing the right thing."

Pilar didn't respond.

"I think you're doing the right thing, or at least you have the right reasons," Marty said. "What I got in my work as a cop and sometimes now at the firm, is a lot of dealings with the bottom of the barrel, the worst fucking filth imaginable, bad people, which is how I know the guy mentioned in the meeting. Just be grateful you'll never have anything to do with that sort of human being, and I use that definition loosely."

Marty pulled up to the townhouse on the beach.

"You know you're too big, too famous, too vulnerable to be living here, right?" Marty asked rhetorically. "Too much exposure."

Pilar sighed.

"So, I've been told. This is the first house I've ever owned, and I love it. And yes, I know I need to move."

She leaned over and kissed him on the cheek.

"Marty, *chao*."

"*Chao, guapa. Hablamos y cuídate.*"

"You speak Spanish?" Pilar asked before getting out.

"Who the fuck doesn't speak Spanish in this town?"

Marty loved to make a woman laugh.

73

Alberto Mejía was typically suspicious of any gringo, and his new friend, although he spoke Spanish fluently, was still something of a gringo. His accent was Spanish with a touch of some other damn language, with the Castilian lisp and inflections Alberto had never heard in person before—most Mexicans hadn't heard a Spanish accent except in movies. Still, he had someone to talk to and so he complained about his illegal status, his fear of *la migra* and ICE, and a lot of the same fears that plagued anyone living without papers.

They'd only met a few times, but they were drinking buddies, an American expression Alberto learned from his new friend, a friend who asked nothing of him and paid most of the time, not that Alberto needed someone to buy his beers. He was also the first person in the USA who'd treated Alberto with respect. With this gringo he didn't feel inferior, like a second-class citizen, like an illegal.

Tag never asked his new pal about his work. He never had to. Alberto gave him an earful about the Greene estate every time they drank together, and the more they drank, the more Tag heard about life at the Greene house.

"You ever need extra help out there?" Tag asked.

"All the time. The wife can't stop changing the landscaping and then expects us to have it in shape the next day. You want on? I can hook it up," Alberto said.

"I don't know. I don't really need anything now," Tag said.

"It pays good. Cash."

"Maybe. Not right now."

"I'll let you know when something comes up. If you want it, it's yours, man. Just let me know."

Alberto called him two days later. Tag told him he was busy for now, then turned him down again four days later. The next time, only a week and a half after they talked in the bar about helping out at the estate, Tag accepted the third offer.

He drove in with Alberto who picked him up at the bar in the morning. At the Greene estate, all of the workers had to check in with the security guard who checked Tag's ID with the name Alberto had given the guard the day before. Not much of a security system, not as far as Tag could see. Literally everyone these days had some sort of alarm system which were mostly useless if people left patio doors open night-and-day so the only barrier to entry was a screen. Greene didn't even have a dog.

Tag found the security at the home to be shockingly lax. He counted seventeen different individuals, between workers and delivery people, who came and went throughout the day, something Alberto said was normal for weekdays.

The richer you are, the more you relinquish your privacy to the servant class.

CHAPTER SIX

Tag was never impressed by the guys from the elite units, or special operations capable (SOCOM) forces like SEALs, or Green Berets, Delta, or whatever. In his mind they were just lifers on a road to nowhere, cowboys and yeehaw hicks who chewed tobacco and had a piss-poor command of the English language. He'd been through Ranger School, which was more or less just a finishing school for non-commissioned officers (non-coms) and officers, something he couldn't avoid if he wanted to be qualified for any decent assignments in either of George W. Bush's two Middle Eastern wars.

He ended up with front-row seats to both.

The elite units required way too much of a commitment, both in time and your personal dignity. The programs selected over two hundred candidates for a class and then washed out all but twenty of them. Tag thought their vetting process for recruits was criminally negligent. From what he'd heard, they basically tortured candidates mercilessly. Tag always hated the hazing bullshit inherent in a lot of military life and refused to participate. He hated being hazed, so why the fuck would he want to inflict this indignity on anyone else?

He'd never thought about doing more than one hitch in the military and didn't want to spend his entire enlistment in training. The truth no one wanted to say out loud was that the best training was in the field. He learned more in a single firefight in the Iraqi desert than he had in Ranger school or basic. You can't teach someone how to keep a cool head under fire, or how to breathe just enough to squeeze off a perfect shot whether at close range or three hundred meters downrange.

No amount of work in the gym can make you tough. Guys who could bench press a piano would drop out on a 10K fun run during PT. The muscle heads were mostly shit at swimming and running and climbing and fighting and almost everything that didn't involve lifting something with a lot of gravitational pull. Most of the tall guys didn't do too well when the shit hit the fan, and in combat the fan was always getting hit with shit.

With major influences from Brazilian jiu-jitsu, hand-to-hand combat had evolved so much in recent years that brute physical strength was almost a liability, as leverage and positioning were infinitely more crucial. Then again, Tag thought, you get two guys with the same training and a fight to the death could be a coin toss. In ten matches, the two might go fifty-fifty, or the other was just too competitive to relinquish a single fight. The problem was you couldn't tap out when the stakes were at their peak, when you were up against a true opponent and not a training partner.

Tag came up against an Iraqi insurgent in some toilet of a village one night on patrol. He entered a hovel two other soldiers had "cleared" when he was hit in the face with the barrel of an AK47. It hurt like a motherfucker, but deflected the round that came out of the barrel a split second later, rendering him deaf and stunned by the noise as well as suffering from the blow to his head, but no mortal blow from a round from this weapon capable of shattering through an inch of solid steel.

He'd already clamped his left hand on the AK47, sending the barrel downward and ineffective. He made the instant decision to let his weapon fall to his side, secured by the sling, trying to disarm his opponent. He easily tore the AK from his hands and smashed the Iraqi with his elbow, a solid blow but not incapacitating. The problem was Tag was encumbered by his rifle on a sling and all the other gear he carried as an American infantryman which included his Kevlar helmet, sidearm, utility belt, vest with five magazines for the carbine and two for the 9mm semiautomatic pistol, a canteen, a lock-blade knife, and a small backpack. Tag felt infinitely overdressed and overburdened.

The Iraqi swung his fist, and Tag ducked his head. The Iraqi howled in pain when he connected with the Kevlar lid of his adversary. The guy was taller and at least twenty kilos heavier than the rail-thin American, so when the bigger man hauled back to strike another punch, Tag stepped into him and wrapped both arms around his midsection directly under the Iraqi's arms while burying his head into the man's chin. Then Tag fell backward on the dirt floor of the hovel.

This gave his opponent the false sense he was somehow winning the contest as he was on top, but the Iraqi had no advantage in martial combat. Tag had his legs wrapped around the insurgent's midsection giving away no leverage. At this point, Tag was focused on his next move, but he was also thinking, "Where in the fuck is the rest of my unit?"

With his rifle, his small pack, utility belt, and other gear stymying his every move, gasping for breath in the stifling heat, Tag rested on his back and waited for his opponent to make his move. The Iraqi was also spent by the suffocating heat, but finally raised his right arm to strike a blow downward.

Tag easily blocked the punch and grabbed his attacker's right wrist with both hands, then spun his right leg over his opponent's left shoulder while pulling on the man's wrist. He managed to straighten out his arm, then swung his entire body around and pinned the man's elbow between his legs creating a fulcrum he used to snap the arm like a chicken wing.

With this damage done, Tag rolled around to the victim's back and applied a choke hold. The man was rendered unconscious in less than ten seconds. Tag left him there on the floor and stumbled out of the hovel, carrying the Iraqi's AK47, his opponent's only weapon.

Choking out an opponent in judo and jiu-jitsu matches never ended in a death because the opponent would "tap out" to stop the pressure, but sometimes someone was rendered unconscious from a choke hold. Quite often, they wouldn't start breathing on their own and required assistance, which simply meant rolling the victim onto their stomach and pressing down on their lower back. This was a minor detail police departments across America failed to explain to their recruits which resulted in a shameful number of wrongful deaths.

Tag didn't care if the guy he'd left in the hovel was alive or dead. He was face down in the dirt and would have to figure it out for himself, so maybe the first guy Tag killed in hand-to-hand combat was in fact one of those "the reports of my demise are highly exaggerated" moments. All he would say was the Iraqi was as dead as Tag needed him to be in that moment. He wasn't out to collect scalps or "kills" unless that meant keeping him or his team members alive.

These days, Tag didn't have a team; his priorities were narrowed down to one person: himself.

In his current occupation in the civilian world, he didn't even have team members to worry about. He was completely on his own, unchaperoned, and unsupervised.

His work was highly paid but didn't require much in the way of skills. Lots of people could do what Tag did, at least most of it.

He followed people, took pictures of them surreptitiously, planted listening devices in their homes, trackers on their vehicles, and sometimes he had to resort to violence. Beating someone up was no rare talent, but few people were willing to step over the lines Tag skipped back and forth across routinely in his job. Most people chose to walk the straight and narrow in life because they rightly feared the consequences of breaking the law.

It wasn't that Tag was unaware or blind to the repercussions of his frequent forays into criminality. He'd served twenty-one months at a medium-security correctional facility in Pennsylvania on a breaking and entering conviction. He knew the consequences of his actions before he was arrested, and he definitely understood them even better after almost two years in lock up, better than most folks outside of a courtroom. If Tag thought he had any sort of talent, he felt he was good at was assessing the odds of a situation, evaluating the risk versus the reward.

He could tell you how much it cost to spend twenty-one months in prison, from what the state paid to house an inmate to how much money he'd lost by not working during his incarceration, to how much someone would have to pay him to languish for another stretch behind bars.

The things Tag did for a living most people would consider too risky for any amount of money, but fear clouded their judgment. Tag understood law-abiding citizens, most people, weren't simply afraid of being arrested, they feared the very idea of many of the things he did for which he was so well paid.

Breaking into a home ran a fairly low risk of arrest, but the very idea terrified a lot of people as this tapped into something more primordial than anything in the legal code. It was simply something decent people didn't do; a thought Tag had heard often enough but never understood. He'd been to war and did a whole lot of things decent people never did, yet he was sanctioned by his government which literally compelled him to violate what most would consider a code of decency.

He'd done far worse things in Iraq than break into a man's car, sit on the floor in the back seat, wait for him to get in, and then frighten the living fuck out of him by popping up and putting a garrote around his neck to articulate all of the horrible things that would befall him if he didn't do as he was told. Compared to war, what he did seemed harmless, although illegal. The difference was in his line of work, a mistake could mean a stretch in jail. In war, it meant your life, the life of a team member, or at the very least a serious injury.

After living with war, being a criminal was just so much easier.

"There's no upside to war unless you count not dying. In this life, the upside can be making a fortune," Tag said to a guy he met who did more or less the same thing for a living.

"Then why don't everyone do this if it's so easy?" his friend said. "It's cause guys like us got the skills to pull this off."

"You think giving some guy a beat down or breaking into his house to steal his laptop are skills? What makes us valuable is most people have a conscience, something I never believed in, or at least never took seriously."

"I'd call that a skill," his friend said.

Tag knew a psychologist might beg to differ and simply call someone with a disregard for the laws of society a sociopath. Tag wasn't qualified to determine if his friend was a sociopath and could only speak for himself. It's not that Tag had no respect for laws, he just looked at it a different way. He tried to explain it.

"Say you're on top of a high building right next to another one but separated by about this much," Tag stretched his arms out to show the distance. "You want to get over to the next rooftop. Most people could easily jump this distance but wouldn't risk it. They'd just walk down the stairs, go into the other building, and walk up to the roof. This risk is minimal, but why would anyone jump across that void?"

"Because they're chickenshit."

"Maybe, maybe not. They don't jump because there's no reward, no upside, or not much. Walking down the stairs and back up's no big deal," Tag said. "That's how most citizens see crime. It's not worth it, all they can see is the risk."

"So, you're saying the average guy don't see the upside like we do?" Tag's friend said. "I never seen it like that before."

"They don't see the upside and they fail to calculate the risk, or at least not properly, and it's a good thing they don't because lots of people could do our jobs, but they choose not to because they fear the consequences."

"Nobody wants to go to jail."

"Of course. Prisons are filled with morons. Hell, I was one of them once. But smart criminals like us, successful ones, we figure the odds. We cover our tracks. We're careful at every step. We don't get caught."

Knocking on wood wasn't something smart people did, but Tag did it instinctively, compulsively. He was an atheist and educated well enough to understand how silly this reflex was, but he was reminded of those Norse graves that had both Christian crosses and the hammer of Thor: they were covering all their bets. At the same time, he rejected Pascal's Wager that it's in a person's self-interest to believe in God because if he exists, you have much to gain, if you don't believe, you have much to lose.

He knocked on wood, but he'd never believed in any god. He knew better than anyone how this was a ridiculous contradiction, but he'd never admit his bit of superstition.

These were the sort of foxhole conversations he had with team members in Iraq, not that they spent much time in holes in the ground. Most of these philosophical discussions were simply a means to combat the intense boredom of life in the tent cities where soldiers spent countless hours with little in the way of entertainment, extremely limited opportunity for sex, and nothing in the way of alcohol.

It wasn't possible to ever win arguments about politics or religion in the army, but they were simply a means for grunts to show off their intellect against the born-again Christian majority making up the ranks. In fact, Tag was the only soldier in his entire unit who had "Atheist" stamped on his dog tags, which prompted a lot of jokes about how he'd be left unburied like a dog because of his blasphemous rejection of the sacred. One of his Christian teammates jokingly made a huge dog tag with Tag's real name, serial number, and a notice: Do not bury, leave body for the dogs. Tag wore the dog tag for an entire day just to show his reverent buddies he didn't believe in life after death and how his carcass was disposed of meant nothing to him.

"Dogs gotta eat, buzzards, too."

And thus, his nickname was born. Tag.

CHAPTER SEVEN

If everything went according to plan, there'd never be a crime committed, or at least one that would be reported. But only a complete fool would ever assume things would go according to any plan, even the simplest or most painstakingly laid out operations never go perfectly. The biggest fear was that he'd be forced into committing a crime that wouldn't and couldn't go without involving the police.

The most probable way for the job to go off the rails would be if the security guard stepped up his usual game and actually did his job. Even this eventuality had been factored into Tag's blueprint, and unless neutralizing the guard or a housekeeper resulted in a homicide, Tag thought it would be in the best interest of the Greene family to keep quiet and make sure the employees kept their mouths shut. Tag was betting he'd have considerable leverage, possibly even enough to cover up killing one of Greene's employees as he doubted the movie mogul valued the lives of his workers.

In the end, it was a three-man job with the driver knowing absolutely nothing about the operation except where he'd drop off the other two, and where he'd pick them up. Another decision was whether to kill both of them after the job. Tag was slightly worried about either of them talking to police after a future arrest and using this operation to bargain their way out of whatever felony they committed that may have landed them in jail. The driver would know almost nothing, and the other, while being involved in the commission of the crime, knew nothing of the client. Protecting the client was everything. Tag wasn't worried about his role. He was a ghost, at least as far as his two accomplices were concerned.

His final decision was killing one or both of them wasn't worth the extra complications and their ability to cause blowback was minimal. How could either of them use this as a way to bargain for a lesser sentence on a crime they might commit in the future if this was never reported to police? Tag was no lawyer but admitting to a crime down the line that had never been reported didn't seem like a plausible move for either of his two accomplices.

If only the two accomplices knew how their lives were decided on a simple matter of logic, of risk and reward, and Tag's knowledge of criminal law as a former prison inmate.

Alberto knew nothing and suspected even less. All he could tell police was he knew a guy and one day he worked at the Greene place. Tag had told him nothing personal, at least nothing that was true. His description would be of a man with a full beard, shaggy dark hair, late thirties, unknown nationality, and he drove an old car. The two hadn't spoken or met in almost two weeks after Tag told him he was moving to Austin for a job. Many in Alberto's life came and went, mostly back and forth across the border, or from city to city chasing work or the rumors of work, or fleeing the immigration authorities.

The driver picked up Tag first, and then the big guy twenty blocks away. Tag and the big guy changed into green coveralls with a logo of a landscaping company on the front. Tag had a small backpack. The big guy just had a pair of gloves and a fleshy mask that would be difficult to distinguish from a human face, at least at night from twenty meters away. In the pack, there were eight pairs of nylon flex cuffs, a roll of duct tape, a few assorted tools, and a high-quality portable video camera.

Inside his coveralls, Tag wore a shoulder holster with a 9mm semiautomatic pistol and three extra magazines just in case the

86

proverbial shit hit the fan. He also had a collapsible steel baton and a lock-blade knife. And if the shit truly hit the fan, he had an M67 grenade, because as any U.S. Army soldier will tell you, it's better to have an M67 grenade and not need it than…Tag forgot the rest. Soldiers said a lot of stupid shit he refused to repeat.

Tag and the big guy both put on their gloves and masks. As the panel van came to a complete stop, Tag slid the cargo door open, they jumped out, then he closed it. The big guy interlaced his hands together and Tag used them to climb up to the top of the van where he took off the two rubber straps securing the aluminum ladder. He pulled the ladder off the top of the truck and jumped to the ground giving the side of the van a slap. It drove away.

The big guy planted the ladder against the three-meter exterior wall. Tag climbed up followed by the big guy who pulled the ladder up and set it down inside the wall. They climbed down, pulled the ladder down without retracting it, and pushed it back, hiding it against the climbing plants at the bottom of the wall. There were motion-sensor lights along the inside of the wall, but Tag had misdirected three of them at that section.

The guardhouse at the main entrance was fifty meters away. The night watchman was sitting in the dim glow of the light inside. He looked to be talking or perhaps singing to himself. They circled around the far side of the driveway, then up the curved staircase on the left side of the mansion's façade. The exterior lights on the front of the house gave off a yellow glow which may have been aesthetically appealing, but the light was inferior to normal electric illumination and kept them from view of the guardhouse.

They moved along the left side of the façade moving away from where the guard was stationed until they came to an open portico with arched columns. As Tag suspected, the sliding inside door to

87

the portico was wide open. He slid the screen door open, and they both stepped inside closing the door behind them. The lights in the downstairs were off leaving Tag to assume the live-in maid had retired to her quarters behind the house.

Tag had never been inside the house, but he knew exactly where he was going. They went up the curved stairs on the left side and made their way along the gallery looking over the living room. Through the closed door, Tag could hear a TV in the daughter's bedroom. He gently pushed a rubber wedge under the outwardly-opening door so it couldn't be opened from the inside.

They kept moving down the interior hallway.

It was just before midnight, a time when Greene and his wife were almost always in bed, but a light on at this hour wouldn't be too unusual. Tag stopped in front of the closed bedroom double-doors and put his ear to one side. Nothing. Tag tried the door. It was unlocked.

One less thing to worry about, he thought. The truth was Tag wasn't much of a worrier, which was a valuable virtue for anyone creeping around in a stranger's home in the middle of the night.

He opened the door and they both entered the bedroom to the sound of the rhythmic breathing of two people in the deepest stages of sleep. There was enough light in the room from the open window to see clearly, at least to discern who was who in the huge bed. The big guy walked around to the wife's side with Tag on the other. The big guy had his hands near the wife's throat, as planned. Tag pulled the pistol from the holster, then turned on the overhead lights.

It took a few seconds before the wife woke up in terror seeing the huge man, a monster wearing a ghoulish mask. The big guy clamped his hands on her throat. Walter Greene woke up to see the muzzle of a pistol in his face.

"Don't scream, don't either of you make a fucking sound, or I'll kill you both," Tag said in a voice just above a whisper.

The big guy eased his hands off of Barbara's throat.

"Both of you nod if you understand."

They both nodded.

"Do as you're told, and you can both wake up tomorrow morning and live your lives just like before. Do you like your lives?"

They both nodded.

"Good. Barbara is going to go to Emily's room. Just walk right in. If it's locked, tell her to open the door. Barbara, your job is to stay with Emily. If you use a phone or trigger an alarm, all three of you will be dead before help arrives. Are we good so far?"

They both nodded.

"Tell Emily you're worried because Walter is on the phone with a big client and it's something about his job. Barbara, you tell her you don't know what's going on and you want to sit with her until Walter gets off the phone."

Tag looked directly into Barbara's eyes.

"Can you do that, Barbara?" Tag asked. "You're a good actor. I respect your work. This is an important role for you."

Tag had scripted that line to achieve full effect: flatter the actor and terrify her at the same time.

"Do you understand, Barbara?"

She nodded.

"When it's all over Walter will come get you. Should be less than fifteen minutes."

The big guy escorted Barbara to Emily's room and removed the wedge he'd placed under the door. He turned the knob. It wasn't locked, and Barbara walked in and closed the door behind her. The big guy jammed the door closed again and returned to the master bedroom.

Tag had closed the curtains and turned on every light. It was now as bright as an operating room, or a film set. Walter was sitting on a chair by the bed in his boxer shorts and nothing else.

"OK, Walter, this is what's going to happen. Do you remember all of the women you've raped over the years? Who knows when you started, maybe when…"

"I haven't…"

Tag struck Walter across the face with enough force to knock out a tooth, but Walter was lucky this time and only had a deep red mark on his cheek.

"This isn't some sort of trial, Walter. You've already been proven guilty. This right here," Tag said twirling the pistol around. "This is me telling you how it is. Got it?"

Walter nodded, a bit of blood seeping from the corner of his mouth.

"We both know you're a fucking serial rapist, something you've been doing for years, hell, decades probably. I've been briefed only on some of the women who you've raped and abused in recent years, women who felt helpless, who felt too powerless to go to the police, women who wanted nothing more than to do their jobs and live their lives. Unfortunately, you stood in their paths, you sick fucking animal."

While Tag was speaking, the big guy took the video camera out of the backpack and set it on the bed. Then he took off his coveralls revealing he had nothing on underneath except for a rather large and very erect penis—Tag had given him an erectile disfunction pill thirty minutes before, and the drug was working as advertised.

"I don't understand what the fuck is wrong with you, Walter Greene, and honestly, I don't care. The women you've dishonored, raped, debauched…Jesus, what the fuck is wrong with you?"

Walter sat in silence.

"Answer me. I want to know. You have a beautiful wife, you are fabulously wealthy, and yet you rape women who work for you. You betray them."

Tag took a few deep breaths.

"If it were up to me, I'd fucking kill you right now, or at least cut off your cock. But those aren't my instructions."

Walter was now sobbing with fear.

"Know what my instructions are from the women you've raped?"

Walter didn't dare to move a muscle.

"They want this big prick to fuck your ass into next week while I get it on film."

Walter could barely force himself to look up to see the big guy who was now kneeling on the bed.

"Now while I have nothing against it, I'm not a huge fan of gay porn, so I think this'll be somewhat unpleasant for the both of us. With that said, Walter, you need to embrace your role as 'the bottom' I think they call it, and act like you really want this. If I think you're unconvincing in your role, I'm going to have to kill your daughter, then your wife as you watch."

Walter sank to the floor.

"I'll kill you, too, eventually, and slowly, just in case you were wondering."

Tag picked up the video camera.

"Action!"

It was all over after a few sordid minutes. The big guy, who'd left on his heavy work boots during his scene, wrapped himself up again in his green coverall.

"Now I just need to upload this," Tag said, doing something with the camera. "Done."

Tag put the camera in the pack, shouldered it, and pointed the semiautomatic once again in Walter Greene's face.

"There's more to this, Walter, if this hasn't been fun enough for you—and something tells me you probably enjoyed it, which wasn't in the plan. If you go to the police, this video will be posted everywhere. You'll be a star, Walter. Do you want to be a star?" Tag asked, with the 9mm in the Hollywood mogul's face.

"No."

"Good, because if you want to be a huge star, just report this night to the police," Tag said. "Got it?"

Walter shivered and nodded.

"One more thing, if I hear one more fucking word of you raping another woman or doing anything shameful and creepy, this video will go viral. And I'll know, Walter."

Walter was shaking with fear.

"Do you have any doubt I'll know if you abuse another young woman whose only desire is to work in movies?"

Walter didn't answer.

"Walter, listen to me. If I hear you've raped another actress, or makeup artist, or production assistant, I'll not only post this video, but I'll come back and kill you. I'll beat you to death with my bare hands and enjoy it."

Tag waited for Walter to recover a bit.

"Walter, tell me if you ever want to see me again, and next time I won't bother with a mask for obvious reasons. I could come over for dinner with your lovely wife and kid."

Walter couldn't even raise his head but shook it slightly.

"Good, so you'll do as you're told, keep your fucking mouth shut, and stop raping women."

Tag turned to leave, then paused.

"Do you have any idea of how much these women hate you? The women you've traumatized and who are paying me to do this? They hate you so much they weren't opposed to killing your wife and daughter to make their point," Tag said.

Walter wilted even further into the carpet by the bed.

"I've done some wicked shit in my life, fucking horrible things, but no one has had this level of rancor for me. What does that say about you, Walter?"

No answer.

"The best thing for you would be to kill yourself. Make it look like an accident, something that will make everyone love you."

Tag laughed.

"Of course, I could help you through that, for a price."

Without another word, Tag and the big guy left the room. Tag sent a message to the driver as they traced their way back over the wall and into the street, leaving the ladder on the ground. The van rolled by with the cargo door open. They jumped in while it was still moving.

Once the door was closed, Tag and the big guy changed out of the coveralls and into normal clothes. He put the coveralls, the masks, and gloves into a paper bag then sprayed lighter fluid all over it. The van pulled off into a strip mall parking lot and cruised to the rear by the dumpsters. Tag lit a cigarette, tossed it in the bag, then threw the bag behind a dumpster. Before they turned left out of the strip mall parking lot, Tag could see the glow of the flaming bag above the dumpster.

Tag was worried about the pistol and the hand grenade, but he didn't want to part with either of them. The M67 was too hard to come by, and the semiautomatic was just a beautiful weapon. He put the grenade, the pistol, the knife, the collapsible baton, and the extra clips into a small nylon bag he had in the bigger bag. He'd toss the bag if they got pulled over, if not, he'd keep it all.

They were still clean items if no crime was ever reported, and even if Greene called the cops, there was no way to link it to Tag. Granted, an unregistered firearm and a very unregistered grenade would pose huge problems if they were found on him, but Tag had a feeling he might need to arm himself again soon. He had a safe spot to ditch them after he was dropped off at a vehicle somewhere way the hell out east on Santa Monica Boulevard.

He drove back west, this time on Sunset. He missed the turn off for the spot where he was going to ditch the weapons, but before he could turn again, he thought against it and decided to hang on to the bag. It was a risk, but he didn't want to lose all of it if by chance someone got lucky and came across his hiding spot. He also thought the spot was too far away if he needed it on the fly for reasons he didn't even want to consider, not now.

The camera he kept. He uploaded a redundant copy of the video, deleted it, then tossed the memory card, just to be safe.

You can never be too careful.

Tag rolled that old chestnut over and decided it was total bullshit. Of course, you can be too careful. People do it all the time, but anyone who was too careful wouldn't have the *cojones* to pull off what just went down at Walter Greene's mansion. Tag didn't even like the word "careful" in the context of his job. He wanted to anticipate and minimize risk. You tell kids to be careful crossing the street, it's not something you say to someone who carries out felonies—sometimes violent—for hire.

***

Walter Greene didn't report the rape to the police, but he messaged his personal attorney and told him he'd come to his office first thing in the morning. Walter's firm wasn't Strauss, Merkle, & Randolf but an even bigger and more exclusive law office in Beverly Hills. Walter drove up to the door of Barrens & Huntley, Attorneys at Law at precisely nine o'clock the morning after, left his car with the valet, and walked in past the receptionist to the office of Charles Huntley III, senior partner and the third Charles Huntley to work at the firm after his father and grandfather who established the office in 1939.

Charles III was a product of Harvard and then Harvard Law and if there was a better example of White, Anglo-Saxon, Protestant, Walter hadn't met the man yet. Even the old family Bostonians and Knickerbockers at Harvard had nothing on Charles Huntley

III. And if two Harvard degrees didn't make him insufferably arrogant enough, he was also a fourth generation Californian. At least this seemed apparent in the eyes of Walter Greene who considered himself a Jewish carpetbagger in LA.

One hell of a lawyer, though, Walter knew.

Walter didn't know for a fact, but he just knew Charles played tennis or squash, or sailed, or did some other silly WASP activity, or at least he looked the part. The only thing that didn't make him feel inferior about Charles Huntley III was Walter was one of his top clients and when he needed a meeting the next morning after texting him at two a.m., he got a meeting.

Walter had already decided to tell Huntley everything exactly as it had happened in his bedroom only hours earlier that day, no matter how humiliating that would be. Greene wanted his motivation to be clear to the lawyer because what he was going to ask him to do would be an even worse crime than he'd suffered.

"Christ almighty, Walter. Are you OK?" was all the lawyer could manage after he finished his story. "Have you been to the hospital?"

What does your savior have to do with this? That was all Walter could think after Huntley's outburst.

"I'm OK. I'm going in for some tests later today."

"How about the police? Have you given a statement?"

"Were you listening? I'm not going to the fucking police," Walter said almost in a whisper. "That's why I've come to see you."

Charles Huntley III finally put things together in his mind as to why Walter had shared this horrifying story with him. On previous occasions, the two men had talked about any future problems Walter may face that had no acceptable legal solution.

"As per our previous conversations, you and I can't discuss this matter any further as it falls outside of attorney-client privilege. We'll have no contact whatsoever."

Huntley wrote something on a small note pad and handed it to Walter.

"How soon can you be at this address on Wetherly Drive?"

Walter looked at the address.

"Right after I leave here, I have one more stop, so after that," Walter said, looking at his watch. "Say eleven o'clock."

"Great. Someone will be waiting," Huntley said while taking a paperback book off a shelf behind him. "Park in the lot and stand by your car. Hold this book like this so you can be recognized."

He held the book against his chest.

Walter almost laughed at the thought, Someone holding a paperback novel in LA would stand out like a beacon.

"The missing number is eighty-six," Huntley said without explaining. "Got it?"

"Eighty-six," Walter repeated, not bothering to ask what purpose this number held.

At eleven fifteen, Walter pulled into the lot. As soon as he raised the book, a bike messenger rolled up.

"Mr. Greene?"

Walter nodded.

The kid pulled a padded envelope out of his bag, handed it to Walter, and rode off without another word. In his car, Walter tore open the envelope and found a cheap cell phone and a piece of paper with a number with two underscores at the end. Walter dialed the number adding eighty-six to complete the sequence. The phone rang. After the second ring, someone picked up and Walter heard a voice.

"Can you meet me tomorrow at seven a.m. right where you are now?"

"Yes."

"Good. You can lose the phone."

"Do I need to destroy…"

The line went dead.

CHAPTER EIGHT

Walter had to move heaven and earth to clear his schedule once again, first for the lawyer visit and the doctor's appointment, and now for this meeting with the guy who hung up on him yesterday. He pulled into the exact same parking spot as the day before at 06:57. At 07:07, a very nondescript four-door sedan pulled up alongside Walter's ridiculously pricey import. All Walter could think was if this guy were working for him, he'd have hell to pay for being late.

Walter had backed into the spot and the sedan pulled in forward so the drivers faced each other.

"Ride with me," he said, backing up to allow Walter to open his door and get out.

Walter got in the front seat. They drove out of the lot in silence. Walter started to say something when the driver held up a hand, making a facial gesture that appeared apologetic, turning something that could have been rude into gesture of politeness. They pulled into a parking garage, stopped on the third floor, and parked next to a wall.

"Now we can talk, Mr. Greene."

Walter didn't know where to begin and had to ask.

"Do you know anything about this matter?"

"Not yet. I just need you to tell me what you want me to do."

Walter didn't need to think about this.

"I need you to kill some people for me. Can you do that?"

The man in the driver's seat didn't react at all to the question.

"That's what I do, or at least part of it," he said. "But let's back up a little. My first responsibility is to talk you out of whatever plan you've been twisting around in your head because it's better to just walk away, no matter what the outcome may be."

Walter didn't respond.

"Do you understand what I'm saying, Mr. Green?"

He was tall, fit, handsome, and dressed casually but expensively: jeans, black leather sneakers, and a T-shirt made to show off his body sculpted to such a degree that most personal trainers would ask him how he did it. Even with all of Walter's training sessions and diet routines, he felt like a slob sitting beside him.

"I understand what you're saying, and I appreciate your concern."

Concern really had nothing to do with his position, the man thought.

"Just so you know, murder is a capital crime and California still has the death penalty, not that they've used it for a while, but I have a feeling they'd put you at the top of the list: Hollywood bigshot in a murder for hire."

"That's only if we get caught," Walter said. "You ever been to prison, ever been caught?"

"Nope. Never been arrested, never had so much as a parking ticket. No fingerprints on file anywhere."

"Congratulations," Walter said with a chuckle. "Wish I could say the same."

"Not getting caught is my biggest priority which is why I want clients to be absolutely certain about what the ask me to do. Crimes of passion are difficult to pull off without having the cops up your ass. Even if there's no proof, the press would devour you."

"The good news is I don't want you to kill my wife."

"That's a good start," the man said. "Let's back up even more."

First, Walter told him about the incident, then about his dangerous and illegal liaisons with women over the years, and how the first thing was obviously motivated by the others.

"So, you have a few women that wouldn't mind seeing you suffer?"

"Ungrateful whores, really. They all worked for me, some of them have made fortunes thanks to my patronage, my guidance."

"Obviously a revenge thing, and it sounds like you have a few candidates that are prime suspects."

He couldn't think of a better revenge for a guy who'd raped women, although Walter never called it rape.

"Any of these women you suspect more than any other? Like maybe one don't like you more than the others?"

Walter sat in silence, thinking more about the incorrect verb conjugation than singling out one of the women.

"We'll get back to that. Anything you can tell me about the men?"

"They wore masks."

"Could you tell if they were White, Hispanic, Black?"

"They were White, the big guy could have been Hispanic, not sure."

Walter told him he was naked except for the mask and his boots.

"Did the big guy have any tattoos?"

"Several."

"Can you describe any of them?"

"I think one was supposed to be Jesus, on his chest, but it was poorly done."

"Was they in color or mostly black ink?"

Walter took a moment before answering, considering again the faulty grammar in his question.

"Mostly black ink, the color ones were poorly done."

"How so?"

"I don't know, like amateurish, I guess," was all Walter could say.

They probably changed some of the tattoos to protect the big guy's identity since he was on film. His tats could identify him more than his face, the man thought.

"Was there any writing?"

"The tattoos?"

"Yes."

"Some writing in letters about this big," Walter held up two fingers to indicate the width. "Spanish, I think."

"Hair color?"

"They both wore black skull caps."

"Accents? Anything you noticed about their speech?"

"The big guy never spoke. The guy with the gun had a slight accent. I couldn't place it except to say he wasn't a native English speaker. Maybe Eastern Europe, but it was very slight. He was articulate, at least I got that impression."

"I need you to tell me as much as you can remember about what he said to you and try to be as precise as possible. If you can't remember, just say so, and try not to invent anything or fill in blanks. Just what you can remember."

Walter told him as much as he could remember, about how the guy called him a serial rapist, about how he had been "debriefed" about the women Walter had raped in recent years.

"So, do you think these women have been comparing notes? Do they know each other?

This seemed to be the first time Walter had considered this. What women? All of them?

"How many women are we talking about, Mr. Greene?"

Walter wasn't the kind to keep score.

"Ten? Twenty? More?"

Walter shrugged as a way of answering.

"So, let's say a number of women. Who were they?

"They all worked for me in one capacity or another. I can't say if they knew each other."

"I'll need their names. All of them."

Walter gave him seven names.

"There were more, but I don't remember their names. It was a while ago for some."

"Can you get the names? You said they all worked for you."

Walter didn't seem too thrilled about this prospect.

"The more information I have, the quicker I can get results."

"I'll do what I can," Walter said.

Walter suddenly remembered something.

"He said his instructions came from the women he said I raped."

They spoke for another twenty minutes about other details of the incident at Walter's home. Walter still wanted them dead. He hadn't been talked out of his desire to see those responsible for the outrage pay with their lives.

The man gave Walter an encryption tool for his computer and an email address where they could communicate via drafts of emails that would never be sent.

"This is the safest way to communicate, I'd bet my life on it. I have, in fact, but this is only for emergencies and to be used very judiciously."

Walter nodded.

He drove Walter back to his car. When they pulled into the lot, Walter turned to the driver.

"What do I call you?"

"Morgan."

The car stopped.

"Listen, Morgan. Do you think I'm overreacting, that this is stupid? Too risky?"

Morgan looked over.

"What they did to you; I wouldn't stop until every motherfucker involved was dead."

Walter was about to open the door.

"One more thing. This doesn't sound like some big mystery. I'm confident I can find out who did this," Morgan said. "I'm good. That's why people like you have my number."

As Morgan drove away, he was already considering who was responsible. From what Walter had told him about his home, it wouldn't exactly take a James Bond type to circumvent the security. Still, it was definitely a professional who'd done this sort of thing before. It also took balls to enter a Beverly Hills mansion in the middle of the night, either that or they were stupid, but the guy who did the talking wasn't.

It probably would have been a fairly expensive operation, something out of the reach of some makeup artist or lowly production assistant who Greene had debauched, although there were other possibilities. Maybe one of these women talked to their boyfriend or husband, maybe one of those makeup artists married some rich guy, some rich jealous guy, or just a man who wanted Walter to pay for his sins. It sounded like Greene made a lot of enemies, and their friends would be his enemies.

The truth was Morgan thought the guy got what he deserved, but that had no bearing on his job. He didn't even give a shit Greene was such a total pig, he just wondered why the guy didn't just pay for sex. A guy like him shouldn't even have to pay, that is, if he had any class or charm at all. He wasn't a bad looking guy, not for his age, but the standards in LA would put Greene on the bottom tier. Good thing he was a movie mogul.

His old lady was pretty hot, too, from what Morgan saw in the recent photos of her. She wasn't active as in film now, and he'd never seen her stuff, but she was legitimately beautiful, even at her age. He was reminded of the old adage: no matter how gorgeous the woman, there's probably a dude who's tired of hitting it.

107

He figured there were at least three involved in the home intrusion, maybe four: the two in the bedroom, a driver, and maybe another covering in the garden or downstairs. Killing a couple of assholes who broke into Walter's house was one thing but offing some A-list actor was another. These days he imagined most actors had full-time security, even some of the lesser gods, and probably all of the women. He didn't want to imagine obstacles that might be in his path, but he hated surprises and he wanted to be straight with his client.

He never said he could do something if he had even the slightest doubt he couldn't, because bullshit like "maybe" and "I'll do it if I can" didn't go over well in his profession.

Morgan had only ever met one person who did what he did, although obviously there were others out there. He wondered if they also were contacted indirectly through high-powered law firms. There could be dozens in LA representing actors. He could probably get client lists of some of them and cross check with Greene's victims, but it was taking a big leap to think this operation was contracted directly or indirectly by a law firm representing the aggrieved actress or actresses.

Morgan wasn't as confident of success as he let on to his client.

***

Her place in Manhattan Beach townhouse was nice, but Marty Evans thought an actor of Pilar's caliber would be better protected in a house with a wall around it. She said she had plans to move soon, but she was never home between work and travel. At least she had parking and a fence around the front. He called her and the parking gate opened. He parked and walked up the stairs to the front door.

Pilar opened the door. Marty couldn't believe she lived alone.

"I hate having anyone in my place, although I have a woman who comes in to clean twice a week," she told him.

"It's time to think about better security, Pilar," Marty said.

"I know. Everyone has told me."

They moved on to the point of Marty's visit. Marty took out a tablet and tapped it to life.

"It's done."

"When?" Pilar asked.

"Last Thursday. No police report."

"Did they get the video?"

"Definitely," Marty answered. "Probably better if you don't watch it, for your own good."

"Hell with that. I want to see him humiliated."

A tough woman, Marty thought. He played the video.

Pilar wasn't quite so tough as she thought she was. She wanted to turn away but forced herself to watch it to the end.

"*¡Puta madre!* How was he afterwards?"

"He was fine, probably enjoyed it. Don't start feeling sorry for that animal."

Pilar didn't feel sorry for Walter Greene, not at all, but violence was something she'd only seen in movies. This wasn't make believe. She sat back in her chair and put her hands over her face and breathed deeply.

"How many women has this guy abused? I guarantee he'll think twice about doing it again," Marty said. "This was the right punishment for his crimes."

Marty knew there were a lot of reasons Pilar Domingo was out of his league, with age and income differences being only two. He wasn't a bad looking guy, especially for a fifty-three-year-old. He was in good shape, but unremarkable for LA standards. He just enjoyed being around such a gorgeous woman, and he liked the fact he was helping her.

"Pilar, I don't have to remind you this is far from over. I don't see any backlash, but you never know how Greene will react."

"What do you mean?"

"I mean, he may not have reported this to the police, but that doesn't necessarily mean he's just going to forget about it. I told you before about how men like him are. He's an entitled son of a bitch, so much so that he thinks it's OK to rape women who work for him, like they're his reward for being successful."

"If he doesn't go to the police, what can he do?" Pilar asked.

"Well, for starters, he knows who did this to him because our man told him. We don't know how many women he's abused, but even if it's a lot, it's a finite number and he knows who they are. Hell, he may keep a scrapbook. A lot of creeps do."

The thought Walter had some sort of souvenir of their episode together made Pilar despise the man even more.

"What are the chances he'll try to…to come after…" Pilar stuttered.

"I'd imagine he'd look into it. As far as making a criminal case against the people who did this to him," Marty said, not mentioning Pilar, "it would be almost impossible at this point, and with every passing day, the chances get slimmer."

"Why is that?"

"It's just the nature of police work. He didn't report the crime, so there's that. He'll never have anything resembling evidence unless you count the film, and Greene doesn't have it, not unless it goes public."

"You think he'll keep his mouth shut? At least as far as going to the police?" Pilar asked.

"Yes, definitely no cops," Marty answered. "But that doesn't mean he won't discuss the matter with someone else."

"Like whom?"

"I can't say for sure. Maybe a private detective, or someone like we hired."

"To do what, exactly?"

"Find out who did it, for beginners."

Pilar gave this some thought.

"Am I in danger?"

Now it was Marty's turn to think.

"If I said 'no,' I wouldn't be doing my job, and my job is to insulate you from this. I studied your deposition from Strauss, Merkle, & Randolf. Your encounter with Greene was quite a while ago and although I'm sure it was horrible for you; it wasn't as violent as what some of the other women suffered by his hands. I think this makes you less of a suspect, at least in his mind."

This wasn't much of a relief for the young star.

"Great, so he's more likely to strike out at one of the other women he actually penetrated."

"Slow down, Pilar. I didn't say he'd lash out. Remember, the very last thing he wants is for the video to go public. Even as a victim, he has a lot to lose."

Marty wanted to change the course of the discussion.

"How soon before you leave this place?" he asked, looking around the townhome.

"Still negotiating for the house at this point, could be six more months."

"Do you need to be in LA, like for work?"

"No, I'm between projects so I'm just catching up on some things, like the new house, and visiting with friends."

"I'd suggest leaving town."

"I've been thinking about it."

"Perfect, I'd suggest the sooner the better, and the longer you stay there the safer it is for you, at least in this initial phase."

Pilar took a draw on her yerba mate.

"OK, now I'm getting paranoid," she admitted.

"Nothing wrong or even paranoid about being cautious. Nothing to be alarmed about."

"Now I'm becoming alarmed."

"Listen, Pilar. I explained this all before…"

"I know, Marty, I know. You did, you warned me, tried to talk me out of it."

"That's in the past, water under the bridge, *agua pasada*," Marty said, showing off a bit of the Spanish he'd picked up over the years. "Now I have a new responsibility and that's keeping you safe and shielded from this. That's what I'll do as best I can."

"I appreciate it, Marty. Whatever you think I should do, I'll do it."

"Then get out of LA as soon as you can, go as far as you can, and stay away as long as you can. Is that possible?"

"I have a break for the next three months, maybe longer as there are delays on my next project. Been thinking about going to Spain."

"Spain's always a good choice. Spent a lot of time there," Marty said.

"I can't believe I've never been. Anywhere you'd recommend."

"Love it everywhere, but Valencia is my favorite. It's great for biking, nice beach, great history, and not too big."

"Sounds wonderful. The truth is I don't even like it here," Pilar said. "I hate to drive."

CHAPTER NINE

Walter didn't tell his wife about the rape. After it was over and the intruders were long gone, Walter showered and sat on his bed in silence for almost thirty minutes before finally seeing about his wife and daughter. He knew he couldn't tell his wife what had happened, none of it. Not only was he too ashamed to say anything, but he'd have to tell her why they did it, that they were acting on behalf of women he'd abused over the course of his career in the film industry. So, he sat on the bed and tried to come up with a credible story to tell his wife.

They were both cowering in Emily's room, too terrified to make a sound or move.

Afterwards, the couple didn't say anything to Emily about what had happened. Barbara had done all she could to remain calm while she waited in her daughter's bedroom. The teen knew something was going on, but she preferred sleep over whatever drama was going on in the house. For once the parents were grateful for their teen's indifference to them.

Walter and Barbara went down to the kitchen to have a drink or two.

Of course, the first thing Barbara wanted to do was call the police, but Walter, without saying anything about the motives of the attack, convinced her their lives would be in danger if the intrusion were reported.

"We're all OK, so let's just forget about this."

"Forget about it? Walter, there were two monsters in our bedroom. How can I 'just forget about it'?"

Walter turned his anger on his wife for challenging him.

"It's because we're in this fucking house," Walter lashed out. "There's no security. The neighborhood is open to anyone with a vehicle. We were warned about the risks."

"That's ridiculous. We live in Beverly Hills. If we aren't safe here, we wouldn't be safe anywhere," Barbara said.

"We're getting out of this dump as soon as possible. There's nothing more to discuss. We could have died tonight."

Walter knew it was ridiculous to think they weren't safe in a multi-million-dollar mansion with private security and alarms, but he swore to himself their next home would be a veritable fortress. He'd never given his personal security much thought before. The only reason they had a full-time guard at the gate was because the former owner had. Walter was an extremely wealthy man, but so were most people in his line of work, some had security, and others didn't bother. It was mostly the famous actors who felt they needed bodyguards, mostly to keep away annoying fans and autograph hounds. People on the business side of the industry had fewer risks and remained almost completely out of the public eye.

Of course, Walter didn't consider this, but he felt a lot like the women he'd abused: vulnerable, exposed, violated, and filled with hate as well as self-loathing. Walter's biggest concern, after realizing the rape hadn't harmed him too much physically, was that he might have a sexually transmitted disease, perhaps even AIDS, but these fears were quickly allayed after a medical exam. He read up on sexual violence and learned the trauma of rape can be devastating, leaving victims in constant fear, ashamed, and plagued by nightmares. The world suddenly can seem dangerous, and you lose trust in others. Relationships change and intimacy

116

with loved ones impossible. There's also the possibility you'll struggle with PTSD, anxiety, and depression.

Not even for a moment did Walter consider the state of the women he'd violated, nor that they didn't have the means to surround themselves with security after their assaults, which is precisely what he did. Three days after the intrusion, he had a team of four security men who would take turns following him day and night, a crack squad led by a former Mossad agent. It wouldn't be permanent, at least not at that level of coverage, but he contracted the team for three months.

More than fear, Walter was driven by rage, by a need to lash out, to strike back, to get revenge. On several occasions, women threatened to report his behavior which made him furious. He swore he would ruin their careers, if they even had a career, or make sure they'd never work in Hollywood if they were starting out, but this was way beyond that. These people, all of them, needed to pay dearly for what they'd done to him.

Who the hell could it be? That was the question. He doubted he could even remember all of them, and certainly not all their names. Trying to get this information for Morgan was proving to be a lot more difficult than he imagined. He began by trying to come up with as many details about some of the more well-known actors with whom he'd had an affair. That was what Walter Greene called his rapes and sexual assaults: affairs. He didn't even consider Pilar Domingo for his list of suspects because their "affair" was no big deal, not in his book. He hadn't asked her to undress, and he barely touched her. She didn't say a word, she didn't cry, she just left. He barely remembered it.

Most of his affairs happened in his hotel rooms when he was traveling, usually to film locations. He'd invite a woman to his room to talk about her career, whether she was an actor, a production assistant, part of the film crew, or even part of the catering crew. He'd be wearing a bathrobe and naked underneath and invite the woman to have a drink with him in his luxurious suite or apartment. What went on from there varied in inappropriateness between Walter exposing himself, touching the woman, masturbating as he talked, to more violent acts including rape.

Some women were able to extract themselves from his advances while many were so dumbstruck by his behavior they froze in terror which Walter considered consent. None of the women Walter assaulted would consider what happened as consensual.

Walter saw things differently, or at least he convinced himself of this. He often did help these women in their paths in the film industry. There were some women who even spoke well of him, although most of these were never subjected to the gauntlet of being alone with him.

On two occasions, Walter was forced to pay off women who objected to his advances. One was some nobody actor, Italian, if he remembered correctly. He was in New York and had met her at a casting meeting for a major production. She was up for a small but significant role, and he let her know through one of his assistants he'd like to talk to her about the part. True to his modus operandi, he'd beckoned her to his suite.

Margarita Bartoni arrived at the appointed time to find the door to Walter's suite wide open. She knocked and heard him call for her to enter and close the door behind her. She walked into the sitting room to find Walter sprawled on a sofa, naked and fondling a pathetic excuse for an erection.

That wasn't the first time Margarita was ambushed by a studio mogul and this time she wasn't shocked, she wasn't cowed or seized with confusion. She was fucking pissed off, furious, and wanted to harm Walter physically.

She let explode a polyglot aria of profanity and threats as she scanned the room for something to use as a weapon, focusing on a vase for long-stemmed flowers which she picked up and hurled at the film producer who was already retreating to his bedroom where he closed the door behind him and locked the door.

"Greene, you piece of shit!" she screamed through the door. "How dare you treat me like some toy. If I don't get that part, I'll report this. Fuck that, I'll kill you, you psychopath, you perverted animal."

She stood outside his bedroom door screaming until she was hoarse.

She received a cash settlement. She also got the part, but she also had to sign an agreement she'd never discuss the incident. According to the document she signed, discussing what happened in his suite would be against the business interests of Overlord Productions and that was prohibited by all employees.

Another production assistant on a set who caused a scene was paid off after her encounter with Walter, enough to pay off her school loans and buy her a house in her hometown in Ohio. But like most serial criminals, Walter couldn't stop, or he didn't want to stop, or he'd convinced himself he wasn't doing anything wrong.

Was Margarita Bartoni correct to label Walter Greene a psychopath? Or perhaps a sociopath? Psychopaths are classified as people with no conscience, sociopaths do have a limited ability to feel empathy and remorse, but often they don't care how their behavior affects others. While professionals might split hairs in defining Walter Greene's pathologies, his sexual predation was certainly anti-social as well as illegal, although no one had ever reported him to the police. Walter took this absence of legal consequences as further proof his affairs were consensual.

Of course, the women felt the enormous power imbalance between their lowly status as aspiring actors or other people in the industry, and this man who pulled all of the strings, the man who made the decisions, who made it all happen.

Now Walter needed to narrow down the list of the women he'd been with who might have done this. Then there was the video to worry about. If it went public, how would it affect him? His lawyer told him there were so many ways to release the video anonymously making any legal recourse hopeless. Once it was out there, that was it. It's not like the video would make the nightly news, but the humiliation…well, he couldn't even think about it. He needed to find the whore who did this. Only then would he feel he'd have a way to make sure the video never went public.

"You can be certain they have some mechanism in place to release the video if they're harmed or killed," Morgan explained to Walter in their second meeting. "The safest bet is for me to interrogate them, forcing them to expose everyone involved. That's how we contain this."

"What do you mean?" Walter asked. "Like torture?"

"No, Mr. Greene. Not 'like torture' but torture, or enhanced interrogation techniques, to put it politely. If I can get in a room with them, it'd take about two minutes for me to make them to spit out the whole story, give up everyone, and figure out how to block the video."

"I'd pay to watch that."

"No extra charge, Mr. Greene."

Walter knew he wouldn't be able to stomach anything like a torture session. He hated violence of any sort; he even despised it in his movies. This was something of an irony considering his aggression against women, but that's not the way he viewed it, not as violence. What they'd done to him, now that was a different matter. It was definitely a violent act and deserved a violent response, something he could never do himself, but powerful men have paid others to do their dirty work since people have been divided by wealth.

Since before the ancient Greeks, champion warfare determined the outcome of conflicts between nations, city states, and anyone wealthy enough to hire someone to fight in their stead. Kings and leaders put everything on the line, betting on a single combatant to do their bidding.

It was a huge gamble, literally between life and death, but it was someone else who paid the price. The rich throughout history have often been able to avoid military conscription by hiring a substitute. During the American Civil War, both the Confederacy and the Union permitted draftees to evade service by hiring someone who was exempt from the draft to replace them, or someone under or over the mandatory conscription age, or someone whose trade or profession exempted him, or a foreign national. The "principal," as those who hired substitutes were called, paid a fee to the government as well as a large sum of money to the substitute. Of course, only the wealthy could afford substitutes. Military conscription during the American war in Viet Nam was geared mostly to snag poorer citizens as university students were exempt, and few of the country's wealthiest young men fought in the war. The sons of the rich and powerful would obtain medical deferments, with a future vice president seeking five deferments to avoid a war he ostensibly supported. A former U.S. President wormed out of Viet Nam by saying his foot hurt.

The rich have always paid others to do their dirty work.

A nobleman in Medici Florence would've walked down the street with an able mercenary at his side. This man was also the leader of the small army in the employ of the nobleman, and he would step in for the nobleman in any case involving violent conflict, whether they be matters of honor or self-defense. Although Walter was the product of the nation's top schools, no one would consider him to be well educated, but even Walter knew something about how historic leaders had hired proxies to fight in their place.

He felt confident having Morgan standing by his side, or at least he was there metaphorically. Walter remembered a name from his first-rate education. Perhaps it was from a history class on Renaissance Italy he'd attended at Harvard, but it could have been in high school, back when he actually read for pleasure and not everything about his schooling was about competition and out-performing everyone else.

John Hawkwood. How did Walter remember that? An Englishman who Walter knew made his bones in the Hundred Years War before moving on to the White Company, a very formidable military unit in the fourteenth century that put themselves at the disposal of the highest bidders. Hawkwood went on to offer his services to Popes and the elite of Florence and Milan.

The name stuck with Walter because he was mesmerized by the fact a man could be so incredibly fearless he would choose to fight as a profession. Walter had always been in awe of military men and warriors because he'd always been terrified of physical conflict. The only other salient fact he knew about John Hawkwood, and the most amazing thing of all was after a life as a mercenary, he died at seventy-one.

He hoped he had his own John Hawkwood at his side with Morgan, but who did his opponent hire? He could still hear the guy's voice in his bedroom, talking in that calm, confident tone, like an airline pilot on the intercom during rough weather as he tries to assuage the terror among the people in the back of the aircraft, keeping them calm while letting them know he was handling the situation. While Morgan came across as supremely confident and competent, the guy in the mask scared the living shit out of Walter. His threats kept Walter awake at night.

"Walter, listen to me. If I hear you've raped another actress, or makeup artist, or production assistant, I'll not only post this video, but I'll come back and kill you."

In spite of his Mossad-led security crew and Morgan, Walter has his doubts as to whether or not he was safe from the man in the mask. If he were determined to carry out his threat, how could he be stopped? As concerned as he was for his personal safety, Walter had no intention of following the man's instructions to keep away from women. He never considered what he did as rape; he had affairs and the women were willing.

He also knew he wasn't capable of stopping. Walter had never smoked cigarettes, but he'd read something about people trying to quit. A psychologist said the first step in quitting was the smoker truly had to want to quit, to live without smoking. It wasn't about willpower as much as convincing yourself you didn't want to do it any longer. Walter didn't want to stop having sex with women outside of his marriage. In fact, he had more sex outside than inside his matrimonial vows.

As terrified as he was of the threats made by the man in the mask, Walter didn't think he was abusing women. Why should he stop?

CHAPTER TEN

"What's wrong with where we live now? You don't like it here?" Emily Greene asked her father when he told her they were moving. Less than a month had passed since the intrusion about which Emily knew nothing at all except her mother acted really bizarre that night. Emily thought it must have been menopause, or she was fighting with her father.

"You'll love the new place more, I promise," Walter said. "You probably don't remember, but you said the same thing about where we lived before this place."

Emily would have been eight years old then.

"No, I didn't. When was that?" she asked.

"You did. Before you had a cell phone, before you were learning how to drive, before you had any interest in boys. Remember?"

She didn't, not even a little. She had her first phone at nine, late for kids in her circle. Barbara and Walter thought they were being firm.

"Mom loves it here. I can tell she doesn't want to leave," Emily said.

That was an understatement, Walter thought. You'd think Barbara had built this fucking house the way she was going on and on about how much of herself she'd invested in it. She met with some architects and interior designers, Walter thought, it's not like she did much of anything substantial, like hammer in a single nail. He assured his wife she could do the same in the new place.

He came across a property that was already being built. The owner was way over-extended and had to get out from under the place. It would be over three times what they'd invested in the ex-rocker's mansion, even with the healthy profit they'd make selling it now that the market was stronger. What sold Barbara was she could actually have input in how the house would be built as it was little more than a foundation at this point. They'd still have to stay within the confines of the original architect's plans, but there was a lot of wiggle room.

Walter would've preferred his own construction project from start to finish, but he was eager to get out of where he lived now, even if that meant renting a place for the interim months while the new place was under construction. Better yet, he'd send Barbara and Emily to their place on Maui, and he'd stay at his favorite hotel in Hollywood. He always got into trouble when he stayed at the Westchester Arms which had the hottest staff of any hotel he knew. And then there were the women who came to his room for meetings. Just the thought of staying there excited the movie producer.

Of course, he knew his daughter would bitch about having to go to Maui. He could hear it already.

"I don't want to go to fucking Maui. I have a life here, in case you haven't noticed," Emily said when she got the news. "Seriously, who even goes there in the summer?"

Barbara wasn't any better at controlling Emily's tantrums than her father. Neither parent had any idea of just how profoundly unhappy their daughter was as they made the mistake of so many of their ilk of thinking giving in to every whim of their child would be a strategy in raising a healthy individual. There was no amount of money, travel, and shopping that could make up for outsourcing so much of Emily's childhood which included private schools, nannies, maids, tutors, tennis coaches, and babysitters.

It wasn't she was such a profoundly damaged kid; she was just typical of almost everyone in her social class and not much different from children of middle class and even poor families, even though rich parents thought their wealth insulated their children from these common pathologies. Emily was obsessed with her phone and the internet, constantly reminded of the fact she wasn't a perfect female specimen, and never able to enjoy what she had because other voices were screaming at her that someone else had it better.

The problems of his daughter didn't keep Walter Greene awake at night. Any child psychologist could tell he thought very little about his offspring, they were low on his list of priorities. Work was Walter's first, second, third, fourth, and fifth priorities. His job and the status he earned from his position was his identity. His family, his wife, his daughter, his ex-wife, and children he had with her meant about as much to Walter—or as little—as books, or films, music, or the daily news. Walter didn't read, watch movies, listen to music, or follow the press.

He'd already failed miserably in his first attempt at fatherhood, barely seeing his children from his first wife since their separation. After the divorce, he saw them two or three times a year for a few hours, putting in the absolute minimum effort as a paternal element in the equation of their upbringing. His first wife, along with her second husband, had somehow raised their two children so they became productive, thoughtful adults, almost in spite of Walter's money.

It was unlikely his daughter with Barbara would avoid the usual ravages of her Beverly Hills peer group. Sometimes called "affluenza," pathologies including drug and alcohol addiction, eating disorders, depression, low self-esteem, anxiety, and other mental disorders. Walter had no idea of his daughter's mental state, he barely talked to her these days between his long hours at work and Emily's retreat into her phone and online shadow life. She had no idea her father was a serial rapist and abuser. His victims were often not much older than Emily, a thought that never occurred to Walter.

A very good question would be to ask Walter what his thoughts were regarding his acts of rape and sexual misconduct. A major contributing factor to how his illegal behavior had become increasingly frequent over the years was the simple fact no one was asking him about them, certainly not the police. Not a single time had law enforcement been involved. Not once was he questioned and, of course, he'd never been arrested. As far as Walter was concerned, they were all consensual affairs with adults.

Walter Greene was the chief executive officer of the third biggest producer of films and series in Hollywood. He was a pioneer in the industry of online content. Granted, he was walking in the footsteps of two other companies that created the industry, forging a bond between the old Hollywood and the internet. Overlord Productions was nothing of an innovator, but they did an excellent job of following the leader and anticipating areas the two bigger online content providers either couldn't fill or directions they'd chosen not to explore.

Overlord began by filling the ravenous need for content with low-budget cooking and travel programs, and moronic reality TV competitions including one short-lived program called "May-December" in which female contestants were paired with potential lovers who were two or even three times their age. From the bottom of the film entertainment barrel, Overlord Productions began to produce content with a bit more sophistication. The big breakthrough came with the resounding critical and popular success of their series, "Thanks for the Memories," a dark comedy about a pre-adolescent whiz kid who turns to a life of crime because he thinks he's missing out on key childhood experiences with his middle-class family.

Walter preferred to talk about other hit shows his company produced because he did everything in his power to cancel *Thanks for the Memories* from the very beginning.

"I don't get it," he said when he first heard the pitch from the writer's agent.

The series was an almost instant hit and Walter wasn't shy at all about taking full credit for the project. Because he'd been cold for the series initially, Walter agreed to a deal with the writer who refused to allow the series to go beyond three seasons, or twenty-four episodes, all of which had already been more or less written. Walter agreed to the contract simply because he had no faith the series would make it beyond airing the pilot.

When the series took off, Walter immediately tried to renegotiate the contract with the writer to extend the series indefinitely, offering more than the initial agreement just to extend the show beyond the artificial limit set by the writer who was infamous for insisting on creative control of his work.

"If you want to pay me more, I'll write you something else, something new," the writer told Walter in an email. "You couldn't pay me enough to run this series into the ground with more episodes. It has a beginning, a middle, and an end. There's nothing after that."

Walter knew there was a lot after that as long as enough people were willing to tune in. He was so furious with the writer he passed on one of his recent novels, a police drama set in Philadelphia with a Black female lead. Another studio picked up the option on the novel from Overlord. They cast in the lead the actor Pilar Domingo who had transformed her role on *Thanks for the Memories* from a minor part into one of the most popular characters in the series. *Twenty-Seven Calls* went on to be one of the top grossing films with a female lead in history. Domingo was nominated for an Oscar for her performance, but in the end, the award went to an aging actor who'd never took home the award before and everyone felt it was her turn.

Overlord Productions was doing so well there was no point at all in dwelling on failures, or things that could have been. Even the worst of their output would make money in some market somewhere in the world. A cartoon series that languished for three seasons in obscurity turned into an unlikely hit when it was dubbed into Hindi and released on the Indian subcontinent.

Even the garbage was turning to gold, and Walter took credit for it all. And why wouldn't he? He'd be blamed if the company went bankrupt. Of course, if it did, Walter and the top corporate executives would make out obscenely well, as was the custom with publicly traded companies. In the current fiscal period, Overlord would release over eighty-six content titles worldwide, up from seventy-two the year before. Eighty-six projects represented thousands of employees all directly or indirectly working for Walter Greene, and because this was Hollywood, many of them were beautiful women.

There were occasions when Walter did actually have consensual sex with women working for him in some capacity. When they came on too strong to him, Walter was turned off, or at least that's what he told himself and he often had sexual performance issues in these episodes. When the women were too forward with him, too eager, too willing, he was intimidated. He couldn't explain it, but he was more turned on when the women were frightened by his advances, startled by his naked body when he ambushed them in his hotel room, or dumbstruck when he groped them during a one-on-one meeting in his office.

Walter was never very sexual. He passed through his adolescence barely conscious of the carnal desires that seemed to be the obsession of every other boy he knew. He didn't even know what masturbation was until he read about it when he was fifteen. He often wondered if there was something wrong with him, if maybe some childhood illness had damaged his sexual organs. His transformation into adulthood came somewhat late and was not particularly vigorous.

Walter was at the very top of his class in high school, at least academically, and in his rather posh public high school in Highland Park, Illinois, that was important. The student body was made up of the offspring of some of the Chicago area's most successful citizens who expected a lot from their children. Like high schools across the country, the athletes were the stars, but at HPHS, the smart kids weren't far behind. In spite of Walter's weak libido and almost complete lack of charm, girls were attracted to him.

If a father was looking for a nice boy who wouldn't debauch his daughter on a date, Walter was that boy, although "nice" wasn't an accurate description of him. He'd grown up being picked on for a host of reasons and developed layers of resentment and anger that simmered just beneath the surface while he struggled to contain them. Walter's attitude partially revealed itself one day in his senior English advanced placement class. This wasn't the first time his resentment toward women had surfaced, but this would be the most public of these displays and the cruelest thus far.

He sat next to a girl he'd known since he was in the sixth grade called Valerie Atkinson. Almost his equal academically and perhaps only a fraction of a GPA point behind him, probably out of the natural tendency for girls to be less competitive. Although they had been classmates for years, Walter had barely spoken to the pretty and bright girl. She was tall, blonde, and Catholic, forbidden fruit for a boy like Walter. They first met in middle school and shared many classes as they were both over-achievers and academic leaders. Walter was immediately infatuated with Valerie, but he was horribly shy and was terrified to speak to her.

When they both began high school at Highland Park, Valerie asked Walter to a school dance in which it was traditional for the girls to ask the boys. Walter could hardly speak after Valerie had asked him in the hallway just after their chemistry class. Too cowardly to refuse the invitation, Walter muttered a weak assent, as if he'd just agreed to give up a vital organ. His shyness terrified him. He didn't so much as look in the general direction of Valerie Atkinson until a week after the dance. She seemed to take the rejection well and never spoke to him about it. In fact, they never spoke to each other except in the class.

Walter's senior reading thesis was on the group of young writers who would be known as the Brat Pack, but only after Walter's high school days. The project required students to read at least three books. Walter chose *Slaves of New York* by Tama Janowitz, *Bright Lights, Big City* by Jay McInerney, and *Less Than Zero* by Bret Easton Ellis. He chose these three not because he was on the vanguard of current fiction but because the page count for all three novels combined was less than seven hundred pages.

Reading fiction wasn't one of Walter's academic strengths. After he finished mandatory classes at Harvard that required reading novels, he never read another work of fiction. He couldn't be bothered to read novels of the movies his studio produced, even the more important ones commanding the biggest budgets. Instead, he had an assistant read the books and give him a five-minute synopsis, like using a human cliff note. Not only was Walter not anyone's idea of an intellectual, he was decidedly anti-intellectual.

By choosing the three shortest novels he could find, Walter had inadvertently become the coolest kid in the class as these three novels were extremely popular at the time. He found all three on the same table at a bookstore in the Highland Park mall.

Valerie Atkinson chose three doorstop novels: *The Prince of Tides* by Pat Conroy (679 pages), *The Cider House Rules* by John Irving (973 pages), and *Lonesome Dove* by Larry McMurtry (960 pages). On this day, students were required to bring their three novels to class to explain why they'd made their choices and to introduce the other student to the books. Valerie's desk seemed to groan with the weight of her three hardbacks, while Walter's three paperback editions together looked like a single selection.

The students were getting settled in before their teacher arrived.

"Dude, everyone knows you're the smallest in the class, but I didn't know that was also the case with your reading material," one of the boys said to Walter.

Mark Kent was a bully and a complete asshole, but he had a sense of humor, although no one in the class found this joke funny. He was tall, athletic, and smart. Not in Walter's league, but he was in advanced English after all.

"Why don't you just do your thesis on three magazine articles, or comic books?"

This follow-up insult got a laugh.

"Dude, check out Atkinson's stack," Mark said.

Valerie had big breasts, so this could've been a double-entendre and undoubtedly was as this was a high school classroom.

"Valerie, any chance you could help Walter out with his, um, size problem?" Mark asked. "Size does matter, even with books."

Mark had three safe selections: *The Sun also Rises* by Ernest Hemingway, *Catch-22* by Joseph Heller, and *The Grapes of Wrath* by John Steinbeck, three books everyone in the class had read in freshman English, including Mark Kent, but there were no rules to what students could choose.

These books would have been an easy target for Walter to ridicule, if he'd had the guts to confront the jock-scholar, but instead he turned his vitriol on Valerie Atkinson who'd done nothing at all but sit at her desk with her three novels.

"Typical Atkinson move, she thinks we get graded on how many pages we read."

Valerie sat in silence, dumbfounded by the attack, much like Walter's later victims wouldn't know how to respond to his aggression when caught off-guard, something that strikes at the heart of a lot of sexual violence. Often, the aggressor is someone the woman knows, and may even trust, so to be suddenly attacked by the man throws the woman into a state of total confusion and chaos.

Most men wouldn't react well when faced with a random, out-of-the-blue act of violence. For very few people, the initial response to any hostile act is to respond with violence or aggression, or even self-defense, not unless they've had adequate training. Sexual assaults are almost always random acts that erupt spontaneously, like a bolt of lightning, or an earthquake.

Valerie Atkinson had no idea how to respond to Walter's aggression. Her first thought was, what did I do? Of course, she'd done nothing, and if Walter had even a shred of courage, he would've directed his anger toward Mark Kent, but his first reaction was to ingratiate himself with his attacker. Valerie hadn't even laughed at Mark's weak attempt at a joke.

The most pathetic thing about Walter's remark was he wasn't finished.

"Maybe you can be president of your book club when you become a housewife."

Once again, Valerie Atkinson was blindsided by this statement so loaded with malevolence and misogyny. She decided it wasn't worth addressing which Walter took as weakness. She wasn't weak or petty or cowardly or passive-aggressive, to name a few things that described Walter Greene. She was simply a well-adjusted young woman who felt no need to insult anyone.

Walter was even more angered Valerie ignored him, turning away to talk to the girl sitting next to her. Her mature way of handling his weak insults tore into Walter deeper than any sarcastic come-back Valerie could have made. He knew—along with all of his classmates—he was a coward for not standing up to Mark Kent, but more than anything he'd wanted to make Valerie Atkinson cry. He began to have fantasies of hitting her, assaulting her sexually. He was a senior in high school and these visions provoked him to masturbate for the first time.

A creep was born.

CHAPTER ELEVEN

Beverly Hills, Brentwood Park, Bel Air Estates, Malibu Colony, Encinal Bluffs, and other hyper-expensive neighborhoods all had one thing in common: they all required spending too much time in cars, at least to Tag's way of thinking. No matter how big your mansion, or how rich all your neighbors were, you still had to spend hours every day commuting to one damn place or another. Tag saw the endless expanse of luxury homes as the world's biggest dick measuring contest, with no apparent winners, or none he could see.

He was being summoned for one of his first jobs in Los Angeles exactly three years earlier. It came through the same Torrance law firm in the strip mall, although they weren't quite as prosperous back then as their turn into the darker aspects of customer service—and big paydays—had just begun. The client was also some bigshot Hollywood asshole, and from what Tag was told and could find out on his own, was involved only peripherally in the movies, some sort of marketing guru. The matter was evidently so personal even the lawyer didn't know what it was about, just that it was urgent, and the client would pay a staggering sum for Tag's services.

How the fuck can I know if I can pull it off if I don't know what I'm doing? A question the lawyer couldn't answer. Why the client wanted to meet at his estate was another unanswered question which explained why Tag was winding up a canyon road into the very upper reaches of Brentwood to the home, a monument to the ego of this marketing guy.

The place, the palace, was absurdly big, Tag thought. Why would anyone want to live in a building that looked like a medium-sized hotel? Tag had met enough stupidly rich people to get the impression they were all completely out of their minds. As he pulled through the gate of the service entrance, he wondered what sort of pathologies he was going to see in this new client. There was a parking lot for at least fifteen vehicles, and this was just for maintenance slobs and housekeepers. For the guests there was probably another lot at least as big on the other side of the property. Tag parked and was immediately approached by a middle-aged man in some sort of butler uniform, he imagined.

"To see Mr. Williams?" he asked.

"Yes."

"Follow me, please."

There was a network of paths along the side of the main house, like rabbit runs for the servants and maintenance people. Tag couldn't even make an educated guess about how many people it would take to keep this enormous estate running properly. There was a small complex about thirty meters from the main house that probably served as the servants' quarters. He followed the servant to a discreet door which he opened and waved for Tag to enter, then he followed behind the guest. It was an empty room with a marble floor that led to a sunken area looking out onto the pool area.

The sunken area was rather sparse, but Tag took it as the guy's office as there was a desk with a laptop computer and a telephone and nothing else. The only other adornments were a sofa with a coffee table next to the floor-to-ceiling windows and patio door. Tag stopped between the desk and the sofa. A door opened and a man entered who looked to be in his late sixties. He could have been sixty or eighty, depending on how he'd taken care of himself in his youth—money can't buy a healthy past. Tag knew Martin Howell was fifty-five.

Tag had seen the type often enough and wasn't surprised, or terrified, but people who've had excessive amounts of cosmetic surgery look like they're wearing masks. They don't look younger; they simply look like they've spent a fortune on plastic surgery.

"Thank you for coming, Mr. Tag," he said. "I'm Martin Howell."

"Just Tag."

The man pursed his lips and probably would have made some sort of facial expression had he been capable of moving any of the muscles in his face.

"Please, have a seat," he said. "Can I get you something? Water? Juice?"

"Oban, one ice cube, thanks."

Tag was never shy about drinking the client's good stuff and not afraid his client would lose respect for his drinking. If a client reproached him for it, he'd walk out the door. He was never reproached.

Howell gave a nod to his flunky who hustled out of the room to fetch Tag his whiskey. Tag half-expected Howell to bark "chop, chop" at his servant.

They sat on the sofa and a moment later the servant returned, put the drink down in front of Tag on the table, and hustled out of the room.

Howell allowed Tag to have a sip of his drink before proceeding.

"I need a man who can get things done. Are you a man who can get things done, Mr. Tag?"

Tag didn't correct him, he didn't get up and leave, and he didn't hit Howell in the face, all things he wanted to do, but checked himself. Instead of being insulted by Howell's remark, he'd simply tack a little something on to his fee. Money can buy a lot of things and Tag's indignation usually could be bought off.

"I get things done."

Howell was expecting more and sat in silence waiting. When he realized there'd be no further elucidation of Tag's qualifications, he continued.

"I need you to hurt someone. Can you do that?"

"Depends who it is. If it's some bigshot Hollywood type, that brings a lot of heat. Guys like you have security, bodyguards, all kinds of things to keep from getting hurt."

Howell chuckled.

"No, this isn't some bigshot. In fact, he's a total piece of shit, a nobody, probably didn't graduate from high school. A drug dealer and pervert. He's fucking my daughter who is all of seventeen. Sells her drugs, too," Howell said. "Can't see what she sees in him."

Other than the fact you hate him? This was hardly the first time Tag had been presented with this scenario. He could probably write a book on the subject of daughters doing horrible things to

140

themselves as a way of punishing their fathers. Low self-esteem mixed with resentment, or hatred, was a dangerous mix.

"The little fucker threatened me. In my own house. He'd spent the night in my daughter's room. I caught him sneaking out the next morning. I blocked his path and he said he'd beat my ass if I didn't get out of his way."

"You don't have security here?"

"I do now. Not then."

"That's good," Tag reassured Howell who was shaking with fear and rage at the memory.

"I just need you to let him know I'm not someone he can fuck with. I need you to kick the shit out of him."

Howell knew next-to-nothing about the kid other than his street name: T-Bone. Just the name was enough to lead Tag to believe the kid was a total punk. Still, if he was screwing Howell's daughter, maybe he had rich parents opening up a host of problems. Even if the parents had disowned their little T-Bone, they might object to someone busting him up.

First things first. Tag needed to find out everything he could on Mr. T-Bone.

"Do you have access to your daughter's phone?"

"Are you kidding? I think she had it surgically attached to the palm of her hand."

"Buy her a new one. Make up a good reason for your generosity."

"She won't care about the reasons. She'll never refuse a new phone."

One less thing to worry about, Tag thought. He told Howell he'd have the new phone delivered the next morning. The deliverer would switch the cards and show the kid the new features of the phone, if there were any. No one would mention the tracking device showing Tag exactly where she was at all times.

Two days later, Tag had everything, primarily the address of T-Bone, AKA Russell McAuliffe, twenty-one years old, born in Stanton, South Dakota. His father was the local preacher until he left in disgrace when his wife divorced him for infidelity. The punk had been arrested once in Los Angeles for under-age possession of alcohol, and once again for amphetamines but not convicted. Tag found no explanations why the charges were dropped. He was living in some shit hole shared house with who knew how many roommates—four, at least—in an extremely unfashionable area off Sunset Boulevard.

How did T-Bone date a girl who must live an hour's drive from his dump? Only in LA could you have a long-distance relationship with someone who lives in the same city, Tag thought.

Tag contacted Howell after he'd vetted the delinquent, giving Howell one last chance to back out.

"Sometimes things go off the rails, go further than the plan called for. Just the nature of this game."

"Fuck that little shit," Howell said as a way of doubling down on his commitment. "Can you do it or not?"

This I can definitely do, especially some nobody dirtbag, Tag thought. Someone the police won't give two shits about, someone no one will miss, with the possible exception of the Howell girl. She'll get over it soon enough. Kids were resilient like that. They bounce back after a tragedy. In fact, she'll probably be sleeping with some other asshole in a week. Maybe another paycheck down the road for him.

He'd have liked to break into where the punk lived and prowl around a bit, get to know him better, but too many roommates, too many unknowns, probably all junkies who never slept, so creeping the joint was out of the question. The place looked positively squalid, like Tag couldn't believe T-Bone and the Howell kid were screwing in that toilet. Maybe they weren't even sleeping together as T-Bone looked pretty strung out.

He was probably just using the Howell girl for her car and the allowance her old man shelled out, five hundred dollars every two weeks. Jesus, for a seventeen-year-old girl! Of course, she was buying drugs. What the hell else could a kid do with that much loot? She was probably buying drugs for everyone in the squat. All that and the little shit had the nerve to disrespect Howell in his own home. Tag thought he could easily teach T-Bone a little something about respect, but that wasn't the assignment. Howell just wanted him busted up.

Busted up he would be…and then some.

Tag had everything he needed. Now he was just waiting around for the right moment to move in and finish the job. No rush, he thought. This was going to be a very profitable visit to LA, but this was it, he swore.

This gig was just too easy to pass up. Big money and not much of a downside. He wasn't worried in the least about the cops. He doubted they'd even investigate. He'd already coached Howell on what to say if anyone came asking, mainly he shouldn't say a damn thing and if he did, it should be through a lawyer. Tag never understood why anyone would ever talk to the police. Stupid people said they had nothing to hide. Everyone has something to hide. Never talk to the police. Period!

There was nothing to worry about. There was nothing connecting him to Martin Howell or Russell McAuliffe. Tag's only worry was the shady law firm, the weak link. If the police leaned on that ambulance chaser, he'd snap once they painted the picture of the possibility of jail time. Not that the lawyer could get to Tag, not directly, but cops can surprise you sometimes.

Most police were fucking idiots but underestimate them at your peril. He learned the hard way. You never know with a good cop, someone with a bug up their ass who won't quit. They could put two and two together to come up with Tag. Some sort of commonality he missed, a description from some do-gooder citizen, a small piece of the puzzle that could snare him. The only thing worse than LA would be a Los Angeles jail cell, or a California penitentiary.

Not much chance of jail on this one. Had the kid been anything other than a complete piece of shit, Tag might have passed on the job and left town the next morning. Hell, he even buffaloed Howell into paying him in full, up front—in cash, of course. He could split and there was nothing Howell could've done about it. It would've damaged Tag's cred in LA, but if he ever came back here, it'd be against his will, or for a career-ending paycheck.

He was staying in a rental apartment he found online, paid cash, no questions asked, and no answers offered. Renters love these arrangements because there's absolutely no chance of the income showing up to haunt them come tax time. Fuck hotels, Tag thought. Even the biggest flea bags asked for ID these days. Tag blamed it all on the pieces of shit responsible for 9/11. They were singularly responsible for making the entire world more fascist and putting more power into the hands of government. Well done, fuckheads. Burn in hell, Tag thought, not that he believed in the concept. How could he with what he did for a living?

T-Bone? Jesus, the kid deserved a beat down just for the nickname. It's one thing when your parents are assholes and give you a regretful name, but when your dumb name is self-inflicted? That's an entirely different level of stupidity.

T-Bone hung out at a dive bar near his junkie fraternity house called The Strip. Tag wondered how many bars had this moniker in LA. He'd wager more than twenty but less than two hundred. If you were looking to buy drugs so stepped-on and cut with innocuous products to the point police would have a difficult time making a conviction in court, The Strip was the place to buy them.

Tag entered through the back door from the small parking lot—every place in LA required parking because, as the song said, nobody walks in LA. The place was just the sort of bar where Tag felt most at home. He'd spent so much time in dives he could probably write a book on the subject, or at least a lengthy magazine article. Rule one of dive bars: stick with beer and shots.

The bartender was a decent looking woman, for her age, Tag thought. For any age, to be honest. That's LA for you. Even a toilet like this bar had a handsome bartender.

"Dos Equis?" Tag asked.

"Sí, señor," the hot fifty-year-old answered.

She opened the bottle and gave him a frosted glass. Nice touch, Tag thought. Between this amenity and the hot bartender, he was quickly reevaluating The Strip, moving it up on his list of favorites.

T-Bone was sitting in one of the booths with two other tattooed, long-haired, and strung-out losers. One or both of T-Bone's companions could have been women. Hard to tell and who cared? Someone else's problem, Tag thought.

Tag had two beers before T-Bone came up to the bar next to him to order a round for the table.

Jesus, if I had a nickel for every hipster covered with tattoos with a beard and a shitty haircut, I'd have a lot of nickels, Tag thought. He heard nickel as a metal was worth more than the coin, but who the fuck wanted a bunch of nickels? It was only four cents better than having a load of pennies and no one wanted pennies. His point was he had no use for guys like T-Bone.

This part wasn't necessary, and Tag knew there was nothing to gain and everything to lose by having contact, but he liked getting a really good look at the people he was after. There was also something about letting them see you that appealed to him.

He looked over at T-Bone. Doing his best to look tough, T-Bone looked at Tag.

"The fuck you looking at?" T-Bone said.

Tag looked away.

146

"Uh huh," Tag said looking in the opposite direction, almost begging the kid to put a hand on him.

T-Bone decided to quit while he was way ahead and went back to his table.

The next time T-Bone saw Tag, well, the boy wouldn't know what hit him.

Tag paid and left The Strip, thanking the bartender and leaving her a big tip, also not a good idea as she'd remember him now, or she'd be more likely to remember him than an average tipper. She was hot; he couldn't resist. He walked out the same way he came in: through the back door to the parking lot. He parked a couple blocks away but wanted anyone who may have been watching to think he drove to the bar. Tag's indiscretion of getting a look at his quarry wasn't much of a risk because the bar was almost full. He was just one unremarkable person among forty people in the bar…and no one saw what he was driving. Maybe when this was all over, he could go back and see the bartender again.

T-Bone never made it home that night, or at least not before 3 a.m. when Tag stopped waiting for him a half block up the street before driving back to his rented apartment.

T-Bone was killed two nights later in a hit-and-run incident which took place in front of his residence. Police determined it happened between 02:30 and 03:00. No witnesses and no one in the area admitted to being awake at that ungodly hour. They recovered a quantity of cocaine on the victim to suggest that he was distributing, or so it said in the newspaper a day later.

Drug related? The police didn't want to open this can of worms and termed it a simple hit and run which looked better for their numbers than an unsolved homicide.

Tag never communicated with Howell after that, but he assumed the concerned father of a seventeen-year-old girl wouldn't have been too upset with the fate of Russell McAuliffe. He wanted him busted up. He got busted up.

Would Howell think Tag's solution to his problem went overboard? The kid could've died from the beating Howell wanted. The difference was that a traffic fatality is almost never classified as a homicide. Had Tag stuck around after running the kid over, the police probably wouldn't have charged him.

Tag shot out two streetlights with a pellet gun before the deed to back up his fiction. He played around with several lines of defense he would've taken if he'd been forced to deal with the police, but that would've been a highly unlikely event. The chances of a patrol car actually witnessing the fatal collision were infinitesimally small.

"He stepped right in front of me."

"The street was dark."

Valid answers to police questions, but it was just too easy to drive away.

He had a contingency plan to have minor body work done on the rental if needed, but he checked and couldn't find any damage. Just to be safe, he went to a car wash and spent twenty minutes power-washing the rental to within an inch of its life. The next day it would be returned to LAX, one of the busiest outlets of the national car rental company where it would go into the pool of vehicles and rented again.

Tag had been thinking about vehicular manslaughter for years. Unless you're drunk or somehow linked to the victim, few people are convicted in automobile-related deaths. It's like a license to kill. He'd read New York City had over two hundred pedestrian fatalities a year caused by automobiles in which drivers are rarely charged with a crime. How many of those were premeditated homicides.

The death of Russell McAuliffe, AKA T-Bone, a drug dealer and addict wouldn't exactly throw the LAPD into an investigative furor. In a week, perhaps less, the case would be totally forgotten, if it's even possible to forget something that never registered in the mind of anyone who mattered. The kid shouldn't have fucked with Martin Howell, a man with the resources to hire a man like Tag.

In Tag's way of thinking, it was a perfect crime. Most people in Los Angeles were more concerned with traffic reports than with traffic fatalities.

CHAPTER TWELVE

There are things more powerful than physical violence, things that can change the way people think and behave that don't involve money or influence or status. Fear. Dread. Terror. These strike deeper into the minds of people and can make them stop dead in their tracks, or retreat, or acquiesce to unconditional surrender. Morgan's most valuable asset, what he did best, was the way he dealt in fear.

Instead of issuing threats that could be traced back to the giver, instead of committing acts of violence which often involved authorities, Morgan used primordial fears to motivate his targets. His method was often a hard sell to clients looking for a much less subtle solution to what they perceived as outrages, attacks against their characters, against their egos. They were baying for blood, for revenge, for pain, sometimes for the death of those who'd wronged them.

Morgan could convince most clients there were more effective ways of making a point than violence. And when his methods weren't appropriate, or ineffective, he had no compunction about going the other way, none at all. In an instant, he could go from attempting to scare someone witless, to shooting them in their bed. Murder for him wasn't a last resort, it was simply another tool in his box. It was a big box.

It wasn't like the old days, and maybe it was never as easy as demanding someone sign a contract or you'd blow their brains out all over said contract. Direct threats could easily land you in prison or facing a lawsuit. Send them a video of their sleeping child with a rat eating peanut butter in their hair with a note saying, "Do as you are told!" and you get people's full attention. Stop an elevator they're on in a parking garage, kill the lights, then call their phone to explain that they should fasten their seatbelts because the cable is about to break, and they take notice, especially if you know they're extremely claustrophobic.

Everyone has a weak spot, we're all afraid of something and Morgan put a lot of effort into discovering these points in his targets, like looking for an open door or a part of a wall that was less secure. Some targets were harder than others, while the most elite, the one percent or higher lived in worlds all but impregnable. Impregnable unless you had remarkably good intel on the target. It was often very expensive information, but the travel itinerary of a fishing trip in Canada made it easy work to take out a business executive on vacation, or the name of a restaurant someone was having an intimate dinner with a Czech model for blackmail photos, or when someone scheduled a private viewing of a sports car at a Los Angeles dealership making a kidnapping almost child's play.

Morgan found these hyper-elites had their own set of weak spots in their defenses, mostly due to the fact they had so many people working for them, from assistants, to secretaries, to massage therapists, to gardeners, to private chefs. Many of these underlings had people working for them. Another vulnerability was many of them were assholes who treated people badly and made legions of enemies everywhere they went. Nice guys may finish last, but those who finish first usually make it there at the expense of others who are more than willing to talk to people like Morgan. For a fee, of course.

Ex-lovers were one of the more fruitful trees in Morgans orchard of intelligence sources. If some of these businesspeople in the most stratospheric levels only knew how expensive some of their discarded lovers were, they'd pay off every single person they ever had sex with and force them to sign a non-disclosure agreement. High-end prostitutes, men, and women, could be even more useful than ex-lovers and Morgan employed a stable of some of most expensive escorts in LA. He never trusted any of them enough to enlist them in the actual gathering of information, but their passive observations were often extremely productive.

Much of what Morgan did could be filed under industrial espionage. He worked with the Chinese who at first tried to hide their affiliation with their government, fearing Morgan would balk at work detrimental to the interests of the United States, or at least American corporations. He taught his Chinese handlers a bit of American slang, Money is green. These days, money quite often wasn't green, depending on the currency, but Morgan didn't let exchange rates or national affiliations come between his personal interests and getting paid.

Not only was he handsomely reimbursed for his work—to put it mildly—he'd also used his insider observations to make staggering coups on investments. Insider trading was the only way to do business, in his mind. He thought the stock market, in general, was like playing a slot machine. He had vices, but gambling wasn't among them.

His few friends, the few who knew even a little about him, advised that a sensible person would retire from his risky profession. How much did he need?

They knew almost nothing about what he actually did. Three of whom were women he was seeing and had no idea about the other two. They only knew it was dangerous, possibly illegal at times, and it kept him away from them for long periods of time. Most of the time he was away from one woman it was because he was with one of the other two, but work did take up a considerable amount of his time, and it always required travel. He could never tell any of them what he did, and the risks he took were as exciting to him as juggling three women in his personal life. The absolute power he felt when he'd vanquished one of these rich pricks was impossible for him to articulate.

He'd stop working when he lost interest in the opposite sex, he thought.

One friend, just an acquaintance to be honest, had a very good idea what he did for a living and had never advised him to quit.

"What would you do? You have no hobbies, no interests. You live for your job. I get it," his friend said.

He did more or less the same thing. Morgan often thought they should work together.

Morgan took the job with Walter Greene simply because the movie mogul didn't blink at the price, a ridiculous fee corporations would pay only because they stood to gain perhaps a hundred times the bill they received. Greene was after nothing more than revenge, something Morgan felt was absurd. The seven deadly sins defined by Christians were lust, gluttony, greed, sloth, wrath, pride, and envy. If revenge wasn't the same as wrath, then it, too, needed to be added to that list. Morgan couldn't knock revenge too much as this was his bread and butter, apart from corporate espionage.

He'd made undeclared fortunes in his career helping other fools in their quest for vengeance and retribution. He often tried to talk clients out of moves he felt were rash and even dangerous, but suggesting they move on, find peace, or grow the hell up wasn't on his menu of services. He didn't sell closure, healing, or redemption, at least unless these sprang from his products of intimidation, extortion, and a varying degree of violence.

Walter gave him a list of suspects, women who he felt could hold a grudge against him. When Morgan questioned Walter at length about each suspect, he heard more or less the same story: it was consensual, he'd helped the women in their careers and they were still bitter, they were ungrateful, they hated men, and all the other things serial rapists probably say. From the rather long list, Morgan felt he could eliminate at least half of them for lack of the financial ability to pull off what had happened to the movie producer.

From what he'd been told by Greene, it was a very professional operation. Now Morgan only wished he could see the video of the crime. If the video was released, Morgan was certain Greene would offer even more to have his vengeance served. Morgan didn't care about saving Walter Greene's reputation or his dignity, but he thought the video would give him invaluable insight into tracking down the culprits. Sooner or later the video would surface.

It seemed obvious whoever attacked Greene in his home had been there before. After spending a few hours on the estate one afternoon, Morgan knew working through the staff would probably yield little. There were just too many of them between the day workers, the deliveries, and routine maintenance people. He counted thirteen on his short visit. He'd have to sift through the women suspects on his list.

He had four very likely suspects, but what Morgan didn't know was his list lacked several names, and one very important one: Pilar Domingo. Had Greene told him about their incident, or more precisely, Greene's sexual assault of the actor, Morgan would have put her somewhere on the top of his list. While Walter told him the man repeatedly referred to the women who sent him, Morgan was skeptical about this being a joint venture organized by more than one person. His instinct told him only one of the women involved set it all in motion.

It could also be a husband or a boyfriend or an ex or even a brother who wanted to teach Walter Greene a lesson. This possibility could expand the list exponentially. He'd have to work with what he'd been given. Although the initial retainer he was working on now was very generous, Morgan was only motivated by the fee he'd receive on completion, a real fortune in itself, and in cash that wouldn't be reported, of course.

Just tracking down the victims on the list would have been a challenge, even for a man in Morgan's position of constantly dealing in the underworld. Having Walter Greene working with you made things infinitely easier. Trying to get a movie star's personal phone number would be a daunting task, just ask any of the creepy stalkers out there dedicating their lives to antagonizing the famous. Walter Greene could get literally anyone who was anyone on the phone simply by asking his personal assistant.

It wasn't as if Morgan could call these women and ask them if they'd hired someone to assault Walter Greene, the man who'd attacked them. Any call to their private line would be met with extreme suspicion and more than likely a prompt hang-up. He knew he'd probably have only chance to get them to talk to him, to give him something he could use toward his objective. He'd start at the bottom of his list, the women with the lowest profiles and probably the least likely to have contracted a professional to carry out a plan of vengeance to do their dirty work.

April Morrison was a makeup artist on the set of a romantic comedy Overlord Productions financed several years ago. Morgan was absolutely certain Walter Greene's version of what happened between them would differ strikingly from what the then twenty-four-year-old would remember. He was certain it was something she'd love nothing more than to forget about completely.

She'd since married, she no longer worked in the entertainment industry, from what Morgan could tell from information supplied by Greene. She didn't seem to be working at all and was perhaps a full-time mother living in Orange County, Mission Viejo to be precise. She must have done well when she was working and saved, or her husband was doing well because their house was a handsome estate.

They weren't rich by LA standards. Almost everywhere else on the planet there would be no other word to describe the couple except wealthy, but April Morrison, now April Riley was living comfortably in the Los Angeles area. Morgan knew she couldn't have financed what had befallen her attacker.

This didn't mean she knew nothing of the conspiracy. She could have been among the women Walter Greene's attacker mentioned, but Morgan had a lot to consider about how he would approach April. He lamented he couldn't use the easiest and most effective way of making someone hand over the truth. He could pick her up while she waited for her son to leave his pre-school, take her to a secluded spot, and she'd tell him anything and everything he wanted in minutes.

This strategy had way too many downsides, unfortunately. This wasn't some total nobody or someone who had something to hide and wouldn't go to the police immediately. She was way too high-profile as a married woman living in an upper-middle-class neighborhood to simply disappear. Morgan wasn't worried about the moral aspects of this scenario, but he was pragmatic in the extreme when it came to his work. Kidnapping and murder were parts of an equation for Morgan that involved calculations on cost-reward. There were way too many negatives in harming April the full-time mom, and the more famous among Greene's stable of abused women were untouchable, at least if he were simply on a fishing expedition to identify those responsible for Greene's assault.

Morgan assumed at least three of the women had shared stories of their ordeals with each other about the producer, perhaps many more than three. This probably meant one of the women was spearheading the crusade. What he needed was better information from Greene if he was serious about hunting these people down. He sent Greene an encrypted message through their anonymous email account.

-Urgent. I need to meet with you. Not in California, needs to be in New York. There now for five weeks.

Greene replied later that day.

-I'll be in NYC on the 15th. Will advise.

Four days later in Manhattan, Morgan picked up Walter as he left his hotel and drove to a parking garage in Midtown.

"I'm getting close, Walter, but I need more from you. More specifics and more names. Some pieces are missing. Maybe you can't remember, or you didn't feel they weren't important, but anything you can give me will speed this up. I can also lean on them to get the video out of circulation."

They sat in Morgan's car on the second-to-the-bottom level in an underground Manhattan garage. It was the middle of the day and there wasn't anyone present among the parked vehicles.

Morgan held up the list of the thirteen names Walter had given him on their previous encounter.

"Jesus, you wrote them down? Isn't that a little risky?" Greene asked.

"Relax, Walter. This list don't mean shit to anyone other than the two of us and this is the only copy. Can you think of anyone, and I mean anyone else?"

Walter gave him another three possibilities although he didn't remember their names.

"I can get them when I'm back in LA."

Morgan didn't recognize any of the names.

"Just assistants, if I remember, or wardrobe people. I'll find out for you."

"Anyone else? Any bigger names? Actresses?"

Walter hesitated.

"I messed around with Pilar Domingo, back when she was auditioning for *Thanks for the Memories*. That was a while ago. You know her?"

"Of course," Morgan said. "I need you to be as specific as you can about what happened between you, Walter. As much as you can give me, as much as you can remember."

Walter described what went on between them, making it sound consensual, as if masturbating in front of a woman you just met could somehow be consensual.

"OK, a big help. Now I need you to take a look at this list and tell me if any of these encounters took place here in New York," Morgan said. "I'm here now so I want to work it from this angle first."

Walter studied the list and pointed out four names. Morgan pressed him for details on each one, asking Walter for as many details as he could remember. Twenty minutes later, they were driving out of the garage and back toward Walter's hotel.

"Two things I've learned never to do in this business, Walter. I never make excuses, ever. And I never make predictions that aren't based on hard facts. With that said, I think I'm getting close. I probably won't contact you again until this is in the bag."

Walter was so visibly relieved he seemed on the verge of tears.

"I'll send you the new communications protocols," Morgan said as he pulled over to let his passenger out.

The new protocol would allow Morgan to delete the account they had used before as an added precaution. He'd also recorded the entire conversation with Greene in the car, complete with High-Definition video. He needed to make the recording in New York instead of California because of the differences in two party consent in recordings. New York is a one-party consent state, meaning only one party has to consent to the recording of an in-person or telephone conversation. In other words, if you are a part of a conversation, you can record without the other person's consent. However, California requires both parties give consent to a recording for it to be admissible in court.

As Morgan pointed out in his first meeting with Greene, he was being asked to commit a capital crime in California, a state that still had the death penalty on the books. It's always wise to have an insurance policy if your client tries to sell you out. While Greene's lawyers at Barrens & Huntley had made the introductions between the two men, no one at the firm would dare be involved in what transpired after. This was unfortunate for Greene because no lawyer would've ever allowed him to have a frank and honest discussion with anyone about his sexual assaults which amounted to nothing less than full confessions. Morgan had many of them now on high-definition video.

CHAPTER THIRTEEN

"Mrs. Riley?"

"Yes," April Riley, formerly April Morrison said, struggling to hold the phone while she was stirring something in a pot in her kitchen.

"Good afternoon. I hope this isn't an inconvenient time. My name is Bob Coleman, from the New York Post."

"A reporter?"

"Yes," Morgan said. "I'm doing some investigating for what I think could be one of the biggest stories to break about Hollywood in a long time."

"What's it have to do with me? I don't even work anymore," April said. "I was a makeup artist."

"This would've taken place exactly four years ago, back when you were April Morrison, working on the set for an Overlord Productions film."

This got April's full attention. She turned off the burner and sat down on a stool in the kitchen island.

Sensing the pause, Morgan continued with his fiction of the reporter.

"This has to do with Walter Greene, the CEO of Overlord Productions."

"What about him?" April asked.

"I've been investigating a series of complaints of inappropriate behavior committed by Walter Greene. Your name came up and I wanted to talk to you directly."

Now April was in full paranoid mode.

"How did you get my name? Who gave it to you?"

"I can only divulge that information if you agree to talk with me."

"About what?" April asked, knowing the answer.

Morgan had her on the hook.

"I'd like you to know our conversation today will be completely off the record. I want to give you the opportunity to think this over before you commit to anything. Without your consent, I won't print your story."

"What story? What do you know?"

"Other women have talked to me, other victims, victims of Walter Greene."

"Fucking asshole. I can't stand hearing his name," she confessed.

"Have you talked with other women; women assaulted by Mr. Greene while he's been the CEO of Overlord?"

April hesitated.

Morgan gave her the names of three women Walter had provided who were also involved in the production of the same film as April Morrison.

"And they gave you my name?"

Now it was Morgan's turn to pause, giving time for April's anxiety to build.

"Let's just say I have your name, Mrs. Riley, and this goes well beyond one film production. I'm talking about a pattern of abuse and violence."

"How long?" she asked.

"Years," Morgan said in his best impersonation of the fictitious reporter Bob Coleman of the New York Post.

"That sick fuck."

"Mrs. Riley, have you been in contact with other victims of Walter Greene?"

She mentioned Kate Barlow whose career had never amounted to much. Then she dropped one more name on him.

"Pilar Domingo. She came to me first. She'd somehow heard of what happened to me."

"And when was this?" the fake reporter asked.

"She talked to me almost immediately after it happened on the set. Then she called me again, this was maybe three months ago."

Morgan was almost too excited to continue. He paused for a moment, as if he were looking over his notes on the other end of the line.

"Why did she contact you three months ago?"

"She just wanted to know if I'd heard other stories about Greene, if I knew any other women he'd assaulted."

Walter had everything he needed from April Morrison-Riley, but he kept up the pretense of the interview.

Morgan's best resource for ascertaining the current location of a top Hollywood star was his client. Walter Greene would have better access to the whereabouts of an A-List Hollywood star than the FBI. He messaged Walter through their arranged ghost email account and received a reply less than an hour later: Valencia, Spain, *Carrer Regne de València* #55602, pta. 18.

Morgan checked the address on the internet and saw it was an apartment building in the middle of the city. On the top floor and by the look of the rooftop terrace, the two upper apartments had been joined together, a nice place but nothing lavish, especially considering Domingo's status in the movie world. She could've bought all eighteen apartments in the building from what Morgan could tell from the reasonable real estate rates in the Mediterranean city of 800,000 inhabitants, the third largest city in Spain.

Morgan not only couldn't speak a word of Spanish, but he'd also never been to Spain which dulled his enthusiasm on finding Domingo's location so easily and precisely. Why couldn't she be in the USA or England? Or Australia? At least everyone there will speak English, Morgan thought. He'd figure it out. He began making arrangements that very day.

Air connections to Valencia were impossible from anywhere in the United States, something Morgan thought was impossible. In the end, he made a better plan by flying to Madrid and then he'd take the high-speed train to Valencia which unlike the airlines, didn't require identification and the security was less stringent leaving no record of his stay in Valencia. He could also book an apartment anonymously and pay for it in cash.

The next thing Morgan needed to find out was the law firm that handled the actor from the Dominican Republic. When Morgan learned Greene had contacted him via a handler at his Beverly Hills law firm of Barrens & Huntley, he thought Pilar Domingo may have worked through her firm to contract the man responsible for the assault on the movie producer. This theory was bolstered when he learned that she was with another law office. Had she been with Barrens & Huntley, it may have been Morgan who was tasked with the break in at the Greene mansion. As far as Morgan knew, there weren't a lot of people in his profession.

Walter had confided to Morgan how he had to tell his lawyer the whole humiliating story of the home invasion and rape that was filmed before the process was set in motion for Walter to be put in touch with yet another, much lesser law firm who then set him up with Morgan. These bottom-feeder law offices were Morgan's conduit to clients looking to solve their problems outside the American criminal justice system.

Even with Morgan's considerable connections in LA, he didn't think he'd be able to be put in contact with the fixer at Pilar's firm of Strauss, Merkle, & Randolf. He knew a bit about that law office, too conservative and careful not to vet the living shit out of anyone

165

they'd steer into their underground world. This didn't necessarily mean that lawyers were careful, but the good ones understood the legal foundation of caution.

Morgan had avoided prison because he insisted on this level of security before a client contacted him, and he assumed nothing less from an exclusive Beverly Hills firm. Walter Greene's firm of Barrens & Huntley had filtered their dirty work through a group of lawyers of the ambulance chasing variety at a storefront firm in Long Beach. The big firms usually insisted on exclusive rights to the best fixers to keep the potential for legal blow-back at a minimum.

Shitbag lawyers using even bigger shitbags to carry out their trash, and I'm the criminal in this equation, Morgan thought. Fucking Walter Greene, serial rapist and hiring out an assassin and Morgan was the guy lurking in the shadows? Incredible, he thought, but that's the way the world worked. Morgan couldn't complain too much. After all, he was rich by most standards, the top ten percent, although out here in Lala Land, his kind of net worth barely raised an eyebrow.

If Pilar's law office had a dirty firm they worked with, Morgan bargained the intermediary at Strauss, Merkle, & Randolf was their lead investigator. Once again, Greene was able to use his influence to find this name for Morgan and from there, Morgan followed up to find out the car he drove. If he had any luck, the tracking device he installed on the ex-LAPD cop's car would lead him to the rogue law office he suspected Pilar's Beverly Hills firm employed when they farmed out whatever work they wouldn't risk doing inhouse.

Morgan soon saw the problem with his plan as Marty Evans was driving several hours a day since the device had been planted.

The tracker logged stops but now Morgan would have to trace the investigator's route to see if any of his stops were at likely law firms, or some other business that might cater to clandestine operations. Most of the law firms Evans visited in the four days Morgan observed were almost as reputable as where he worked, but there were three much lesser firms that seemed on the shady side. After three more days of monitoring the investigator's movements, Morgan thought a small law office in Torrance was a match: Bishop and Sharp.

It didn't take much digging for Morgan to uncover that while the little firm appeared prosperous, they were lower-tiered lawyers, ambulance chasers who were either working night and day, or they had their hands in negotiations that paid well above their usual legal fees. Both lawyers had impressive homes in Brentwood, so either they'd married well, or they were dirty.

Marty Evans was coming to the Torrance office at some very strange hours for legal work. Typical cop, or ex-cop, Morgan thought. Evans was too arrogant to think anyone would ever follow him. As a cop, he'd done all of the hunting. He didn't bother to lock his door at night, as if daring anyone to threaten him, to enter his world. Evans never changed his route to the Torrance office allowing Morgan to know his destination as soon as he got on La Cienega Boulevard.

Evans was on his way there now.

Why was this ex-cop visiting shady lawyers at nine o'clock in the evening? It was sketchy enough for Morgan to believe he'd identified the Beverly Hills law firm's link to the nefarious underground world where he worked. He wondered if this Bishop and Long had their own fixer and if he was any good. From what Greene had told him of the intrusion, the guy was good, definitely good enough not to get caught. Even if Greene had reported it to the police that evening, Morgan doubted they would've had much to work with.

Morgan started making his way there from where he was staying in Hollywood. He'd arrived at least twenty minutes after the ex-cop so he was hoping his business at Bishop and Sharp would keep him there long enough for Morgan to intercept him at the strip mall. If not, at least he might be able to find out which of the two partners Evans was dealing with at the firm.

Morgan arrived at the strip mall thirty-five minutes after Evans who was already heading back to Beverly Hills, but he was in time to see Roland Bishop closing the door and heading to his vehicle, German and expensive, of course. Bishop was the one who looked like a lawyer while the partner, the tax guy, looked like an accountant, both right out of central casting. Morgan would try to follow him home but tailing people in LA was a pain in the ass, to put it politely.

Bishop drove like a teenager and left Morgan at a red light after only four blocks.

Morgan knew it wasn't worth it to press it in this situation. He'd tag Bishop's BMW so he could track his every kilometer just looking at his computer and without risking being spotted or pulled over by the police. Trying to follow him tonight might have saved him a little time, but Greene's thing wasn't exactly time sensitive, except Pilar Domingo's stay in Valencia, Spain, where she was staying in a very vulnerable location in the city, perfect for Morgan. But first, he needed to be sure she was the correct target.

Morgan had a command decision to make. If this were the right guy, Roland Bishop could clear up a lot of loose ends for him. All he needed was to have a little talk with the ethically-challenged counselor who was living way beyond the means of an attorney of his ilk. Morgan would normally have weighed the extreme consequences of his next move a lot more carefully, but the pay-out on this job warranted the very calculated risk.

Once Morgan had delivered the verdict on the low-life lawyer, his only concern was not getting caught. Bishop's well-being, his family, his life didn't enter into the plan, and the plan was very simple.

He needed to peg Bishop's car with a tracking device, see where he went for a few days, find a spot to intersect with the lawyer, then have his conversation.

It only took Morgan four days of tracking the lawyer to find a pattern and then his weak point.

In this case Roland Bishop's weak point was parking for his gloriously expensive German sedan he refused to leave on the street in Venice when he stayed at his new girlfriend's place. He paid to leave it in a lot two blocks from the young woman's shared bungalow where he paid the rent for the twenty-eight-year-old yoga instructor. Morgan had no idea if Bishop's wife knew or cared about the fact her husband of fifteen years and the father of their two children was slumming it on the beach a couple nights a week, but he imagined it would have been news to her.

How many times had this cliché been repeated in the city of angels? That of the young professional on the rise who realizes he married too soon. Morgan wondered why a guy like this would get married at all. If you like to screw around, screw around, he thought, but why get married unless you're really sure about that path? It was fitting Bishop's little love intrigue was going to cost him a lot more than the young lawyer could have ever imagined.

Morgan had someone working with him on this evening, a driver of a panel van parked between the lot and the yoga instructor's bungalow. Morgan hadn't fully vetted Bishop and for all he knew, the lawyer could've been a national judo champion, or he could just be a crooked lawyer who allowed his cock to get him into a lot of trouble. Morgan's back-up would make sure the operation didn't go south right out of the starting gate.

The starting gate in this case was the side door to the panel van opening as Bishop walked down the deserted street. Morgan pointed a sawed-off shotgun in the lawyer's face as he racked in a round. In a truly tactical situation, the shotgun would have had a round in the chamber and ready to rock-n-roll, but the sound of a shell being racked into a sawed-off was a real attention-getter.

"Keep your mouth shut, do as I tell you, maybe even tear off a piece of ass later tonight instead of me putting a round in your face."

Bishop stopped dead in his tracks.

"Get in the van. We need to talk."

Bishop got in the back. Morgan followed, shutting the sliding door as the van drove off. Morgan pushed Bishop to the empty floor.

"Hands behinds your back."

"What's this about?" Bishop finally said.

Morgan hit him on the side of the head with the barrel of the sawed-off.

"Hands behind you and shut the fuck up."

Morgan secured Bishops hands with nylon flexicuffs. He secured the cuffs to the side of the van. Then he pulled Bishop's keys out of his pocket. He placed a length of duct tape over Bishop's mouth that had a small hole enabling him breathe freely, then a blindfold.

"Any sound out of you and I'll fill your mouth with sand. Got it?"

Bishop nodded.

"Good. Play by the rules and you go on with your life."

The van stopped. Morgan gave Bishop's keys to the driver who got out of the van and walked to the parking lot where the lawyer had dropped off his pride and joy bit of German engineering. Morgan drove the van.

The next thirty minutes of driving represented the biggest risk of the entire operation that evening. Getting pulled over for a routine traffic stop would've triggered a desperate reaction on Morgan's part, the only way out during the commission of a kidnapping, a crime that can be prosecuted on the federal level with a possible life sentence, and in some cases the death penalty.

Morgan drove calmly. He was relaxed, with barely a hint of an adrenaline buzz, something he enjoyed but knew from previous experience this sort of high could be dangerous. It often caused over-confidence when caution and restraint were more appropriate. Getting pulled over was highly unlikely at this point, but the grave danger of that unlikelihood tempered his every action.

"Fifteen minutes, Mr. Bishop. Relax. A few questions and you'll be on your way," Morgan shouted back to his unwilling passenger. "Safe and sound."

Morgan made a somewhat circuitous route to his destination just in case Bishop tried to estimate the location in his mind. The van pulled into a workshop in a grimy industrial area of South Los Angeles. The automatic door opened but no light was visible inside. When the door closed behind the van, Morgan got out and turned the overhead lights revealing a mechanic's studio the purpose of which was difficult to discern. There was a wooden table built into the wall on the left side with tools on a pegboard above it. The floor was bare concrete and covered with oil and paint spills.

Morgan helped Bishop to stand up and exit the van, his hands still cuffed behind him and the blindfold still in place. A chain dangled from the ceiling that Morgan attached to the nylon cuffs. Morgan pulled on the other end of the chain and Bishop's arms rose behind his back as he stood as erect as he could. When he winced a bit in pain, Morgan stopped raising the chain, then lowered it a notch to relieve Bishop's discomfort keeping him on the balls of his feet.

Morgan was behind his prisoner.

"This is it, Mr. Roland Bishop, esquire. This can either be very easy or unspeakably difficult, up to you. I'm going to ask you a few questions, and you answer to the best of your ability. If I think you're telling the truth, you walk out of here, back to your wife and kids, the big BMW, and the yoga instructor in Venice."

Morgan gently took the duct tape off the prisoner's mouth.

"I hear anything other than what I think is the truth…"

Morgan wanted this to register.

"Anything else and the last person you will see in your life will be me, and you can't even see me."

Then he took off the blindfold so that Bishop could see around the filthy workshop.

"Does this shit hole look like the last thing you want to see in your life?"

A very short pause.

"No," Bishop whimpered.

"How do they say it in court? Do you promise to tell the truth, the whole truth, and nothing but?"

Bishop nodded.

"Say it."

"I do. I'll tell you the truth."

"So which way will it be? The easy way or the other?"

"The easy way," Bishop begged. "I want the easy way."

Morgan read up enough on the subject of interrogation to know torture didn't work, except when it did. If you were looking for information that could be verified immediately, it worked. For example, you ask someone for the pin number of their bank card as you are about to cut off one of their fingers as you stand in front of an automatic bank machine. They'll give you the number.

However, if you ask anything that can't be immediately verified, a trained operative will spill out a load of nonsense. A guy like Bishop, who thought his life now depended on telling the truth, had little motivation to protect anyone by trying to resist, and if he did, he'd soon change course when pressure was applied. Morgan didn't have to so much as slap Bishop's face for the lawyer to answer every question he'd prepared. Bishop even improvised on his questions and filled in a few more blanks.

Morgan learned it was Pilar Domingo who'd contracted her attorneys in Beverly Hills to find a solution for her problem. The ex-cop, Marty Evans, turned out to be the intermediary, and Domingo had insisted on speaking with Bishop, against Evans's wishes. It got rough for a while when Bishop said he had no way to get in touch with his fixer, presumably the man who carried out the intrusion at the Greene mansion. Morgan hyperextended Bishop's left elbow, a move that was extremely painful but would leave no outward marks. In the case he left his hostage alive, Morgan didn't want Bishop to have anything that needed explaining, like a broken nose or a severed finger.

Bishop told him the fixer contacted him, and not the other way around, never the other way. If he needed work, he'd contact Bishop in some manner and they'd exchange encrypted emails, or he'd arrange for Bishop to receive a phone they'd use.

That's about the way I work, the way I was taught, Morgan thought, taking Bishop at his word. At least he had a very good description of his rival fixer. He had Bishop tell absolutely everything he knew about the man, which wasn't much. What was instructive for Morgan was Bishop's recollection of their meeting together at his firm when they met on a Sunday morning less than two months ago.

"You did well, Roland," Morgan said in closing. "I videoed this whole interview, or whatever it was. None of this could be used in court, of course, but anyone seeing this'll know you're into some very nefarious shit, things you wouldn't want brought to public attention."

Bishop didn't object.

"The best thing for you is just to forget this ever happened. Not a word to anyone, especially to that fucking cop, Evans, or ex-cop" Morgan said. "Got it?"

"Yes, sir. I got it."

Morgan was going to leave it with that but thought a bit of added insurance could do no harm.

"I planned on killing you after this, that's why we took your car from the lot. Give anyone looking for you a bit of a curveball so they won't know your last location. We're not sparing you out of the goodness of our hearts, just doesn't serve us at this point. We get word that you're making a fuss; you won't even see us coming the next time. Understand?"

Bishop nodded.

He didn't see them this time.

Morgan drove Bishop around a bit then had him get out, still blindfolded, in an empty parking lot.

"Leave the blindfold on while you count to sixty. Your car, phone, and wallet can be found at the address on the paper in your coat pocket. Have a nice life."

Morgan sped away while Bishop stood counting out loud.

CHAPTER FOURTEEN

In the three weeks since arriving in Valencia, Pilar hadn't driven once, she hadn't even taken a taxi. She'd flown from LAX to Madrid, and from Barajas Airport, she took the metro to the main station of Madrid-Chamartín-Clara Campoamor where she caught the AVE train (*"ave"* meaning bird and in this case the acronym for *alta-velocidad*, or high-speed). Ninety minutes later, after racing at up to three hundred kilometers an hour across the high plains and tunneling through the mountains of Castilla-La Mancha she stepped out of the station in Valencia's historic center.

She was traveling with a girlfriend from New York, both carrying a single rolling suitcase and a small backpack. After checking the location of the flat they'd rented, they decided to walk—a preposterous concept for anyone who's ever lived in California's biggest city...or anywhere near it. The two friends planned to rent a car, but their first transportation decision in Valencia set the tone for the rest of their stay in Europe: no cars.

Their apartment was on postcard-perfect boulevard lined with ornate apartment buildings dating back to the first decades of the twentieth century and shaded by tall date palms and acacias, and on top of that it was only three blocks from the train station. The accommodation might not have impressed most A-List celebrities, but Pilar Domingo hadn't forgotten her humble roots in Santo Domingo, not yet.

By any normal standards for the majority of the planet's citizens, the penthouse apartment, with its huge terrace, would have been positively sumptuous, and so thought Pilar and her friend, the actor Carmen Giménez, now called Carrie Gold. Carmen was from Guanajuato, Mexico, but she'd lived in Los

Angeles since her parents came there when she was four years old. For both of the Latina actors, this was their first time in Valencia.

"I think I'm gonna like it here," Carrie sang as the two walked into their new home for the next two months.

Carrie hadn't achieved anything near the level of career and financial success as her friend, but Pilar was new to the superstar thing and still clinging desperately to her humble past. She'd witnessed, first-hand, people self-destructing from stardom and she vowed to never allow that to happen to her. She'd give it all up before she'd let Hollywood bring her down.

Riding a bike in LA anywhere other than the beach was as hazardous as most war zones. With cars driving at excessive speeds, distracted drivers, and the murderous aggression of commuters, riding a bike was filled with peril in Los Angeles, and on most roadways without bike paths where cycling was permitted, it was just short of suicidal.

This was why Valencia was such a revelation for Pilar. There were bike paths everywhere in the city. Directly in front of her apartment building, there was a separated bike trail down the handsome boulevard which went to the historic center of the city, and if you rode in the opposite direction, you'd end up at the city beach of Malva-Rosa.

"I may never drive a car ever again," Pilar said to Carmen as they rode leisurely around the city center early one Sunday morning, the silence so complete when the bells of the cathedral rang out, Pilar could feel the vibrations on her clothing. Cars were becoming an endangered species in Valencia's historic district thanks to a vigorous campaign by the local government to pedestrianize all of the major squares. At the same time, the town hall was working feverishly to squeeze out automobile traffic and limit on-street parking throughout the city

From the vantage point of his rented sedan, Morgan found it impossible to follow the actor and her companion in the city center. Valencia's Turia Park was also car-free, but Morgan had less trouble surveilling the pair when they rode to the beach, or other areas of the city. They were easy to follow as they had their rented bikes parked in front of their building and usually left each morning at about nine o'clock, an odd hour for a Hollywood star, Morgan thought, assuming they stayed out all night and slept well into the afternoon.

He confirmed with Greene before leaving for Spain, convincing the producer Pilar Domingo had orchestrated the attack against him. He lied to Greene when he told him he was close to identifying the men who actually carried out the crime. It was a mix of wishful thinking and optimism on his part, and Morgan's intention was to question the actor at some point to learn more about the assailants. The lawyer told him she'd never met the fixer, and Morgan was sure he was telling him the truth, but perhaps he didn't know the whole story.

Extrapolating from his relationship with Greene, it was possible Pilar Domingo met with her fixer, too. He wanted to get into her flat and have a look at her phone or computer to track down the video of Greene's assault.

Getting into her holiday flat was almost too easy. Morgan entered the building next door, went to the top floor, broke the lock on the door to the roof, and from the roof it was a simple matter of scaling a small barrier separating the two buildings. Once he was on the roof of that building, he only had to jump down a little over two meters and he was on the deck of Pilar's apartment, and as he suspected, the patio door wasn't even locked.

He couldn't find a phone, not that he expected as much. Who leaves the house without their phone these days? There was a single laptop computer, password protected and unbreachable. Even the FBI couldn't break these barriers without the direct cooperation from the manufacturers, which they were loath to give. He took photos of the belongings of both women for no other reason than Greene might ask him to prove he'd attempted to recover the video, even though Morgan told him the video was a lost cause, like trying to put a genie back in a bottle.

Morgan had assured his client the video was probably on several computers as well as stored on the web somewhere, at least that's how he would've done it. It could be automatically set to be posted on a public forum at a certain date which could be changed as that date approached. This would insure if the person who wanted the video posted were eliminated somehow, the video would make its way to the public. Efforts could be made to take the video down, but by then, the damage would've already been done. You can't un-release a viral video just like you can't push back a tsunami.

Morgan had discussed the video with Greene, but until he'd seen it, there wasn't too much he could say.

"Just prepare yourself; it'll leak out sooner or later."

"Then what am I paying you to do?" Greene fired back.

This asshole, Morgan thought. Good thing he's paying me a fortune, or I'd teach him some manners.

"You're paying me for revenge. That I can guarantee; the video's another matter."

Morgan wasn't as sure about the vengeance angle, at least not back when he made his promise to Greene. He could guarantee some poor slob somewhere would be held accountable for the attack on the movie producer, whether that person was guilty or not. If Morgan couldn't hunt down those responsible, he'd find a patsy and sell the fiction to Greene as fact. Greene would feel his honor was defended—or whatever he felt needed defending—and his check would clear.

Morgan was upfront and honest with Walter Greene about the possibility of squelching the video, but he swore to do everything possible. His chances of eliminating it were zero, he couldn't even imagine how that could happen in the age of instant digital reproduction with one mouse click sending it into the wild blue yonder of internet infinity.

Walter Greene, you'll need to embrace your fifteen minutes of fame, Morgan wanted to tell him.

Right now, looking at Pilar's laptop with a privacy protection system that would stymie NSA experts, Morgan's initial assertion about hunting down the video was only reinforced. At least he had proof to show Greene he'd made extraordinary efforts in that direction.

It would've been easy enough to just sit in the dark and wait for the two women to return later that evening. Even if they came back with a couple of men they'd met out on the town, he could slip away without being noticed. However, as much as he would've liked to interrogate the actor and make her give up everything she knew about the video and the assault, a double homicide would simply be too messy, especially in Spain where murder was practically unheard of outside of domestic violence situations, and many of those committed either by elderly Spaniards, or foreigners from Latin American countries or Eastern Europe, as that old-world, sexist violence had dropped propitiously among younger Iberian men.

Two women killed in their home in this city would create a news cycle. The murder of an incredibly famous woman and her friend would generate a shit storm of truly epic proportions. Even if this were to be the last job Morgan ever carried out, there was just way too much exposure for that kind of crime—and he liked what he did. Retirement wasn't anywhere on his horizon. Morgan didn't have any idea of what that would even look like.

He had no interests outside of his work. If anyone asked, he'd say he didn't have time to read, watch movies, or listen to music. He liked women, but he'd never had a relationship that had lasted more than a few months. His work came first, and he traveled extensively, although he avoided flying whenever possible to avoid records. He liked money, loved it beyond most other things, but spending it generally gave him little pleasure. Although he drank on occasion, it was nothing approaching a vice. He wasn't particularly attracted to good food and never understood what all the fuss was about when people raved over new restaurants. If he had a choice, he'd prefer to take a pill rather than eat.

His biggest thrill, his vice, was his work. He knew most people would be absolutely terrified to break into a stranger's apartment, but he thought they'd all be electrified by the enormous thrill it generated. Was it better than sex? Absolutely, without a shadow of a doubt. Anyone who'd ever done both would probably agree.

Killing another human being was something that provoked an even bigger rush of adrenaline and whatever other chemicals the human body produced to articulate extreme pleasure and satisfaction. Morgan had learned this when he was still a child.

Morgan's father was a mystery even to his own mother. She lived paycheck to paycheck, if you could call it living, working as a waitress and turning the occasional trick. They were living in a one-bedroom dump in Dayton, Ohio, a city Morgan felt was about as bad as America could get. When he finally traveled, he understood how wrong he'd been.

His mother brought home a customer from the restaurant where she worked with the promise of a night cap and perhaps more. What his mother was too stupid or too drunk at the time to understand was what really caught the interest of the forty-six-year-old out-of-towner was when she mentioned she had a teen son at home, so they'd have to be quiet.

Morgan was asleep on the sofa in the cramped, sweltering apartment and hadn't awakened when his mother came in with her latest guest, as she called them. The man leered at the boy sleeping face-down in his underwear as the couple made their way into the bedroom.

After a failed attempt at intercourse, and his mother's adamant refusal on a refund, the man closed the door to the bedroom, wedging it closed with a folded bit of a newspaper.

Morgan was an adolescent, but strong and tall for his age. And although he was handsome and intelligent, he'd been picked on mercilessly for his lowly economic status and his mother's reputation. He had a chip on his shoulder, he had grudges to settle, and he'd been described by a school guidance counselor as "prone

183

to violence." The counselor had no idea of even a fraction of what was lurking inside the mind of the boy.

When Morgan awoke, the crime had already been committed, although technically it wasn't a rape, there'd been no penetration. The creep had finished with Morgan in a matter of seconds, if that, then dropped over onto his back in exhaustion, like they were lovers. Morgan reached out for the first thing he could lay his hands on which was a glass ashtray he used to batter the skull of his abuser repeatedly until he'd made a hole in the top of his head big enough to pass his fist through.

It was very a messy death; a mistake Morgan would never make again. Guns and knives were fine in warfare, but unless you were trying to make a statement with a killing, there were much better methods than shooting and or stabbing.

The boy washed the gore off himself in the bathroom, got dressed, and opened the door to his mother's room to find her passed out naked on the bed.

"Get up, we gotta get out of here," he shouted. "Now!"

The light shone brightly in the front room. Through the doorway his mother could see the bloody corpse which Morgan had pulled on to the tile floor as he immediately began the disposal process. The kid had watched a lot of crime movies and TV shows about criminal investigation.

Morgan wrapped the corpse with garbage bags, mopped up the blood as best he could, and threw the bloodied sheet covering the sofa into another bag. His mother pointed outside to where the man's car was parked only a few steps from their front door. With her help, they carried the body and put it in the trunk.

Morgan and his mother didn't exchange a single word as they packed what was theirs and left. The mother and son had only been in the apartment for five days. She'd paid cash for a two-week stay and no identification was asked or offered. There was nothing that would indicate a crime had been committed in the apartment, although their panic-stricken clean up wouldn't stand the scrutiny of a thorough police investigation. However, if no one suspected the man had been there, there'd be no reason to look.

His mother had worked only nine days at the restaurant where she met the stranger. No one would miss her, and no one would care she'd left without notice—such is the impersonal nature of lousy jobs. It was highly unlikely anyone would remember she left with a man on her last night at work, especially since everyone involved in the place drank more than was recommended. It was just another night of excess.

On their way out of town, Morgan drove the man's car and left it in a parking lot of a shabby apartment building—he'd learned to drive, at least a little, two years earlier. Morgan had wrapped the body again, this time with two plastic leaf bags he'd emptied from a dumpster with the hope of cutting down on the odor that would signal the cops. The longer the body remained undiscovered, the more difficult was the work of police investigators. Any fan of cop shows knew that.

While carrying out the onerous task of getting rid of a body, he found a little over three hundred dollars in the man's front pocket—every little bit helps when you're going on the lam. He got a decent watch out of the crime as well as a few things from the car before he and his mother drove west out of the city, not stopping until they were two states away from the scene.

They never heard anything about the case ever again and never returned to Dayton.

Morgan had just turned thirteen.

This was when he began his home schooling, but since there wasn't much in the way of schooling, and he and his mother often didn't have a home, it simply meant he stopped going to public school once and for all. Education comes from many sources, and for Morgan, those were mostly of the criminal variety. He was a star pupil.

CHAPTER FIFTEEN

A hit-and-run accident leaving one dead and one victim in critical condition was a news story that would make the headlines in Valencia, but wouldn't travel further, unless one of the cyclists was an international film star. The first reports said that Pilar Domingo was pronounced dead at the scene of the accident which took place at six-thirty p.m. on a bridge over Valencia's Turia Park.

The scene of the accident was total chaos as the car had driven over a divider into the bike lane, striking the two cyclists from behind and scattering their bodies, bikes, and belongings over a distance of fifty meters. The women's bags were thrown well away from the broken bodies, explaining the misidentification of the deceased, which in the end was Carrie Gold, formerly Carmen Giménez. Pilar Domingo was put into an induced coma, a common procedure in cases of severe head injury. She was receiving the best care possible at Valencia's *La Fe* Hospital, one of the largest in Europe.

Morgan returned to the United States and was safely through customs before he heard anything about the unfortunate accident on the bridge. He wasn't too upset to learn the fatality was in fact Carrie Gold and not Pilar Domingo, as previously reported. He was certain his client wouldn't be disappointed with the way things turned out, and Domingo was far from out of the woods.

The best part was that, although there'd be an investigation, it would come to nothing as there was nothing to suggest foul play. The car he used would never be found, and if it were, there'd be nothing linking it to the accident. Accidents happen. There was even the chance that Greene's video would never surface. Now the only piece left in the puzzle was finding the man who made the video. Unfortunately, Morgan had nothing to go on, not a thing, not even an idea of how to proceed.

Marty Evans had a very good idea of how he was going to proceed. He didn't believe in accidents or coincidences, and he didn't think for a split second what happened in Valencia was anything other than an assassination, and the only person he felt had sufficient motivation was Walter Greene. He'd warned Pilar of this from the moment she explained her plan of retribution against the serial rapist.

Evans's job was to look out for the interests of Pilar Domingo as a major client of the law firm of Strauss, Merkle, & Randolf. Her plan of vengeance against Greene was well outside the firm's purview, but Evans was told to look out for her as best he could. Along with that responsibility, he'd grown quite fond of Pilar, and was extremely sympathetic to what she and the other women had gone through with the movie mogul.

With the aid of one of his younger, more tech-savvy assistants, Marty uploaded the video of Walter Greene's sex tape to every video portal on the internet. Many of those posted on reputable video sites would be taken down almost immediately, but not before hundreds, if not thousands of views were captured around the planet. The pornographic websites would keep the videos online until they received actual court orders for removal. The video was posted with the caption, "Movie producer Walter Greene getting his freak on with a masked lover at his Beverly Hills mansion."

Marty Evans knew dozens of reporters from his years on the LAPD force, and he sent several of them the video "anonymously." Within twelve hours, the video went viral to the point of breaking the internet, as people said. The video appeared to depict a consensual sex act, especially the part where Greene performed fellatio on the big goon wearing the mask. Walter had oversold the part where he was ordered to make it look like he was enjoying it.

Walter Greene had not prepared his law firm to deal with this crisis, and they weren't used to being hit with anything this big standing flat-footed. Had they been in the loop, their people could have done a lot in the initial hours to protect their client. The Los Angeles Times wouldn't touch the story, not until they'd fleshed it out a bit, but the lesser vultures in the world of pseudo-journalism tore into it like hyenas on a baby gazelle, as did the Hollywood blogging community, some of them going as far as reposting the video.

"Make them stop this," Walter screamed at his lawyer. "Sue them all. Have you read any of this shit?"

Walter scrolled through his phone.

"Behind-the-Camera Producer Becomes a Star. Walter Greene's Smash Debut in Gay Porn. 'Love Me Long Time,' Says Walter Greene, CEO of Overlord," Walter continued hysterically. "You Go, Baby. Can the Wife Be Jealous if it's with Another Man?"

Walter read another half-dozen gutter press headlines.

Charles Huntley had a stack of periodicals on his desk. He'd obviously seen the stories.

"There's only so much we can do. Trying to shut down these blogs is like chasing shadows. There is literally nothing we can do

189

from a legal standpoint. Of course, no one is going to claim responsibility for the video."

Walter sat back in his chair in Huntley's office. Although he was devastated and humiliated by the release of the video, the timing hadn't come as a surprise: less than twenty-four hours after the news broke about Pilar Domingo's almost fatal accident in Spain.

Completely against his will, Walter Greene was now a star known around the world. The clock was ticking as his fifteen minutes of fame had begun in earnest.

Marty Evans wanted nothing more than to keep Greene in the limelight, at least until he was sent off to prison. He also wanted to hunt down the piece of shit who killed Carrie Gold and possibly Pilar as well. In all his years of police investigations, he'd never felt such relentless fury to bring down a perpetrator.

First of all, Evans wanted to know how anyone could have known Pilar Domingo was involved in the Greene affair, unless you believed in coincidences and thought her hit-and-run was just a random accident. His first thought was the shabby little strip mall in Torrance. He made an appointment with Roland Bishop after normal hours at his law firm.

Marty entered the office at nine p.m. on a Tuesday, walking through the empty offices to Roland's spacious quarters at the back. He closed the door behind him.

"Who'd you tell, Roland?"

Roland sat behind his desk with a glass of whiskey in his hand, caught off guard by the question and Marty's vehement tone suggesting he wasn't here to play games.

Before Roland could get the word "what" out of his mouth, Marty had struck him across the mouth with his open hand, knocking the drink from his hand and almost pushing him out of his chair. Marty put on a pair of brass knuckles disguised as a cartoon figure, not even made of brass but heavy plastic—one less thing to worry about from metal detectors while delivering the same punishment as the standard variety.

"The next time I hit you, Roland, you're really going to feel it. You won't recover, not completely."

Roland believed the threat.

"Some guy came and asked me about what happened to Greene. Tortured me. I had to tell him…at least what I could."

Marty smashed his brass-knuckled fist down on the keyboard of the laptop on Bishop's desk, shattering it into pieces with parts striking Bishop in the face.

"He tortured you?" Marty asked. "What did he do? Show me the scars."

"He said he was going to kill me," Bishop stammered.

"You just said he tortured you. Did he threaten you or torture you?"

"Threatened me…hurt me."

Marty punched Bishop in the thigh, making him howl in pain.

191

"Shut the fuck up. I didn't break anything."

Bishop tried to keep quiet.

"So, some thug threatens you, and you give up Pilar Domingo to this animal. Do you know what happened to her?" Marty screamed.

"Yes."

Bishop hadn't laid eyes on Morgan and had nothing to give Marty that would help him find the man responsible for Carrie Gold's murder and Pilar's life-threatening injuries. What he learned from the cowardly lawyer was the tragedy in Spain was no random accident. He may have been chasing a phantom, but at least he wasn't simply working on a hunch, and Marty was certain that Greene was behind the assassination attempt.

The ex-cop did the same backtracking that led Morgan to the law office in Torrance. He looked for his peer in Walter Greene's law firm of Barrens & Huntley. As it turned out, he knew the man, at least peripherally, through their shared service with the LAPD, a former detective by the name of Tom Winchester. After a phone call or two, they met at a bar in Beverly Hills.

"Who's your fixer?"

Marty began bluntly.

"Fuck you, Marty. Who's yours?" his opposite demanded.

"You willing to give me five hundred thousand dollars if I do?"

Tom started to laugh but caught himself immediately when he could see Marty wasn't joking.

"Hard to get ahold of. Total psychopath, scary fucker, truth be told," Winchester said.

"Do I look scared?"

"Just saying. I sell him out, he's coming for me."

Marty heard enough about Tom Winchester to know he was a hard-ass cop who'd put dozens of vicious thugs in prison, any one of whom would've loved nothing more than to harm the man responsible for their time behind bars. It was the nature of police work, which was why he took Winchester's words very seriously.

"I give you my word, Tom. If you give him up, I'm going to dedicate my life to burying this fucker."

Marty placed a folded bit of paper on the table between them. Winchester picked it up and read the dollar figure.

Tom Winchester realized this wasn't some idle boast, and a half a million dollars in cash was a life-changing opportunity. As far as his allegiance to the firm of Barrens & Huntley…well, he was willing to risk it. He thought he could have his cake and keep his position even though he'd be violating a half a dozen company policies as well as a couple of the non-disclosure agreements he signed. The firm would never go public on the matter of having a fixer, if not on their payroll, then on their speed dial, so any legal threat against him would wither if Tom took the case to court.

Delivering Morgan on a platter was a boast he couldn't make, but he was certainly willing to do everything he possibly could. Contacting the person calling himself Morgan was like conjuring a genie or summoning a ghost from the netherworld. As a gesture of good faith, where "good faith" was the small matter of a half a million dollars in unreported cash, Winchester confessed to Marty he'd brokered the meeting between Walter Greene and his firm's fixer of last resort, the man who'd do almost anything for a fee. Just what Walter Greene paid Morgan was a secret to which even Tom Winchester wasn't privy, just as he had no idea of the business conducted between the two parties until Marty Evans informed him.

"You don't need to know anything about the procedure, but I can't just ring this guy up," Tom said.

"I figured that much. Just set it in motion and let me know," Marty said.

Winchester posted a message on a site which he was only able to view once every four days. Morgan would either respond or he wouldn't. He wasn't always available to serve the needs of the law offices of Barrens & Huntley in Beverly Hills.

"There's a distinct possibility he retired. If he did what you claim, Greene must have paid him a bundle," Winchester said.

Marty knew enough about this type to understand they never retired; they either ended up in prison or dead. There was no magic number they had in mind for their bank accounts where they'd ride off to a beach somewhere and find a hobby. Morgan did whatever he did because he got off on it. The fact he could get paid handsomely for it was just dumb luck.

Another thing about which Marty Evans was one hundred percent certain was that Walter Greene had his own way of communicating with the killer for hire. The two were, like it or not, indelibly joined together over the murder of Carrie Gold, an unfortunate bit of collateral damage in Greene's attempt on the life of Pilar Domingo.

"Think maybe he'll try again?" Tom asked. "Finish her off?"

Marty had thought this over.

"Wouldn't make any sense. She may not pull through, and if she does, she's looking at a long road to recovery. The Spanish police have nothing on the case, and it stands as a simple hit-and-run. He makes another attempt, they'll see it as an assassination, clear as day. Not much of an upside."

"You're probably right."

"I hate to say it, but the hit and run thing was a brilliant move. Shit, even if he got caught, he'd never serve time. How often did you see a prosecution in a vehicular manslaughter case, let alone an actual conviction?" Marty asked.

"Never, unless the guy was shit-faced drunk. Sober, it's just an unfortunate accident. Maybe the guy pays a fine," Tom said.

Marty had recently reviewed the statute in California, California Penal Code Section 192(c), which defines the crime of vehicular manslaughter as driving a vehicle in a negligent or unlawful manner and thereby causing the death of another human being. Unless a prosecutor can prove the defendant was using his car as a weapon, or the death was caused by gross negligence on the part of the driver, convictions are hard to obtain and jail time is almost unheard of.

He made a cursory search of the Spanish laws and their legal system seemed even more lenient toward vehicular homicides.

Even leaving the scene of the accident was only a matter of three to six months in jail if there was a conviction. The Spanish police had made no progress in the case. No vehicle had been found, there were no witnesses, and the sole survivor was still in critical condition and if she did recover, there was little hope she'd be of any use to investigators.

While he waited for word from Tom Winchester's attempt to contact the fixer, Marty only had a name: Morgan, and he didn't know if that was a first or last name.

"Marty, be prepared for some good news," Tom Winchester said over the phone the next day.

One hour later, they met at the same Beverly Hills bar.

"You never know what you have on your computer. I really need to be more careful as there's probably stuff on here that could sink me," Tom Winchester said as he turned his laptop around and pushed it across the booth to Marty.

Marty pushed the PLAY button, and the video began. It was only a few seconds of a tall man walking into a room and sitting down at a desk, but the video quality was excellent.

"Forgot I had this. First time I met our Mr. Morgan. Thought I might need a mug shot. Used the video camera on my laptop."

Marty would have preferred to have the man's location, but a high-quality video clip was a lot more than just a name.

"Thanks, Tom. How's it going in the other department?"

"Left a message, and I can check it tomorrow. Not much else I can do."

There was plenty Marty could do with what he had now. He sent the video clip to the *Policía Nacional* in Valencia, explaining there was reason to believe this man, who may go by the name of Morgan, should be considered as a suspect in the hit-and-run murder of Carrie Gold. He knew it wasn't much, but he'd made many cases with a lot less in the beginning. Marty knew the Spanish police didn't have a prayer of making a case against Morgan who'd probably left the country hours after the murder, but it would be useful if they found evidence he'd actually been in Valencia.

CHAPTER SIXTEEN

Marty Evans had done everything he could to talk Pilar Domingo out of her revenge plan against Walter Greene. She wouldn't waver and was more motivated by the harm the producer had inflicted on other women than by her own disgusting encounter with the creep. Although Marty couldn't convince her to change her mind, he was able to impress upon her the dangers of embarking on her plan of assaulting a very wealthy and powerful man.

"Forget about going to jail over this, if he somehow discovers you were behind it, what do you think he'd do?" Marty asked at one of their preliminary meetings.

"Don't know. What do you think?"

Marty had thought about this considerably.

"I think any man capable of doing the things he's done to so many women is capable of murder. I've seen it too many times as a cop."

"I'll just have to hope he doesn't find out," Pilar said.

"Hope is a shit strategy, pardon my bluntness."

While Marty wasn't one to panic, he thought the best thing was to have her see all the cards on the table.

"He'll probably come after you. Why wouldn't he?"

Pilar was a little less confident than she was a moment earlier.

"I'll do everything in my power to insulate you from this, but there's always the distinct possibility of a weak link, of someone selling out, of exposing you," Marty said.

"What? You think he'd try to kill me?"

"Definitely."

Maybe she was just acting, but Pilar seemed strong and confident once again.

"I've thought about this for months. I want this motherfucker to pay for his sins. I'll just have to accept any consequences."

Her sangfroid was admirable, but now Marty was nervous.

"What if you end up dead all of a sudden? A drug overdose or something that looks like an accident?" Marty asked.

This dark turn took Pilar by surprise.

"You think he'd do something like that?"

"You have no idea the things powerful people are capable of doing. I'm not sure nice guys finish last, but they don't rule the world."

"Then I'll need another plan. Can you make that happen?"

"I could."

With help from her law firm, Pilar set up a special account that would be activated if she died or was gravely injured and incapable of guardianship over her own affairs. Marty would have access to the account.

"Almost two million dollars. That's a lot to trust anyone with," Marty said after the agreement was drafted and signed by all parties.

"I hope it never comes to it, but I trust you'll carry out my wishes," Pilar said.

Once again, Marty wasn't able to dissuade the actor from this latest amendment to her plan, reminding her of the end result of taking an eye for an eye.

What he really wanted to tell her was she should just have Greene murdered and get it over with, once and for all. That would be the only way to guarantee he'd never rape another woman again.

Another amendment to Pilar's agreement in the case of her death or injury was that her deposition concerning Walter Greene's sexual assault would be made public. If she died, there was little chance that her videotaped accusations against Greene would lead to an arrest as prosecutors were loath to bring charges against a defendant unable to face the accuser. It's hard enough to win a conviction in cases of sexual assault when you have a great witness, but the memory of a victim doesn't carry much weight.

Pilar Domingo was still fighting for her life when her lawyers presented her statement to the Los Angeles County District Attorney, which fortunately was where the alleged assault took place six years ago. If nothing else, the story made the day's headlines—and the lawyers purposefully chose a slow news day.

In their statement, her representatives asked other victims of Walter Greene to come forward, promising Strauss, Merkle, & Randolf would represent them all, free of charge. This was slightly disingenuous as their fee would be part of Pilar's agreement with Marty if something happened to her. Many of his victims were wealthy women completely capable of launching their own legal assault against the lecherous CEO of Overlord Productions.

Less than twenty-four hours after the announcement, seventeen women came forward with claims against Greene. Some were unknown players in the movie industry, but eight were names anyone who'd watched movies in the past few years would recognize, and three were stars to the point of being household names.

Walter Greene was on the defensive, on the ropes, attacked in so many directions that his law firm, which was without equal, was falling to its knees.

"We're finished, Walter," Barbara Wilson told her husband. "I've known you were a piece of shit for a long time, but…what the fuck! You're a serial rapist?"

They were living in a temporary mansion as Walter managed the move between the ex-rocker's place and the new, ridiculously opulent place in the last stages of construction.

"It's all bullshit," Walter countered. "Jealous cunts who didn't get what they wanted."

A very poor choice of words on his part.

Walter was still spinning from his sex video and all of the repercussions from that nightmare. For the first time in his life, Walter felt his professional career was in jeopardy, something that had always fortified his ego in the face of his many other shortcomings. Walter was a winner, the valedictorian, the top earner on Wall Street, the biggest producer in Hollywood, or at least one of the biggest. What now? Arrested? Jailed? Ruined?

The most famous of the victims speaking out against Walter Greene was Valentina Margoli, an Italian actor who'd starred in one of Overlord Productions' most successful limited series. She was twenty-two years old when she was cast for *La Frontera Saga*, a Mexican drug war epic where the cartel paid taxes on their earnings directly to the rural poor of northern Mexico. She loved the politics of the story and was thrilled to be cast. She was ambushed by Greene as soon as she left the office with the news she had the part. She hadn't reported the crime but told her agent about the sexual assault. She'd also compared notes with Pilar Domingo a year after the incident.

Rumors immediately circulated about Walter Greene's possible involvement in the hit-and-run accident that had taken the life of Carrie Gold and placed Pilar very close to death. Marty Evans fed the story of Greene's connection to the same internet jackals posting the producer's sex tape. When Valentina heard about Pilar's horrible accident, she asked around. Even if the rumors weren't true, it was enough to infuriate the Italian actor and she immediately reported her rape to the LAPD.

Like Pilar, Valentina Margoli had grown up poor and had seen her share of hard times—as in rural Italy hard times. She was tough and accepted the indignity of her sexual assault. She knew she had little to gain and everything to lose by denouncing Walter Greene, but that was then, when her career hadn't even begun.

She'd already made more money in the past few years than her entire family had made over the course of their entire lives. If she never worked again, she'd be just fine, more than fine. She had everything she ever dreamed of as well as the ability to provide for her relatives. Walter Greene didn't have any power over her. In fact, she could see he was getting weaker every day as he tried to explain away the sex tape, and hers was now the fourth sexual assault claim against him.

The really bad news for Walter was Valentina was a great actor and her accompanying press conference after she spoke with the Los Angeles District Attorney was the performance of a lifetime.

"When I was at my most vulnerable state in this city, when living paycheck-to-paycheck would've meant I actually had a paycheck, when I was sleeping on a sofa and eating leftovers from my friends' fridge, I landed my first major role in the series *La Frontera Saga*. My elation was immediately shattered when I was sexually assaulted by Walter Greene, the CEO of Overlord Productions.

"Of course, I didn't feel I could report the heinous crime, and neither could I ever forget about it, as hard as I've tried. Only now do I feel myself in a position of sufficient power and independence to report the attack. My biggest regret is my silence has allowed Walter Greene to remain in the sewer and out of the light of justice. I apologize sincerely to all the women he has violated, who also felt too powerless and too ashamed to protect themselves or report his crimes.

"I'm no longer a poor artist desperate for work, the ingénue Walter Greene attacked in an office on the lot of one of his productions, and I vow to do everything in my power to make sure he doesn't prey on another woman."

Walter Greene knew his situation was dire, to put it mildly. There had been accusations in the past, but none of them were ever made public, especially this public. His lawyers struck deals involving financial settlements attached to non-disclosure agreements and the women had disappeared. Greene's wife had not heard anything about her husband's sexual misconduct, or she chose not to hear.

He and his wife were to make a joint statement about the night the intruders entered their bedroom. They'd explain how the video was made at gunpoint with the culprits threatening to kill Greene's wife and teenage daughter if he didn't do as they said. The joint husband and wife press conference had been scheduled two days earlier, but a lot had happened in the previous forty-eight hours. Four accusations against him had made headlines in the past week just as he and his lawyers were trying to contain the forest fire of his sex tape scandal.

Barbara Wilson accepted the fact her marriage was little more than a mirage at this point. There wasn't a shred of romance, or sex, or the slightest physical attraction between the two of them, not for years. She suspected him of indiscretions. She'd heard a few rumors of worse behavior on his part she'd ignored. As many women do in similar circumstances, she told herself her priority was holding her family together, of providing a stable home for their child. She thought when their daughter moved out of the house at eighteen, she could move on to another, happier chapter in her life.

She'd been staying at their estate on Maui instead of living at the house Walter had rented temporarily while waiting for the completion of the mega-mansion. Walter had been calling her frantically when he found her flight from Maui to the Burbank airport was not on the list of scheduled flights.

"Where the fuck are you, Barbara? I need you and Emily at this press conference," he screamed into her voicemail.

This was his fifth message after her phone had gone directly to voicemail on each call.

Just so Walter wouldn't think something happened to his wife and child, Barbara sent him a brief text message.

"After you get all of your rape trials sorted out, maybe we can talk."

Some of Barbara's closest friends had asked her about her marriage and how much she was willing to endure for the sake of her daughter and her exalted status as the wife of one of the city's top producers. What was her limit? When was enough, enough? She could never answer the question before and swore to the people in her most intimate circle things weren't that bad, as many people do who live in barely tolerable situations.

Four public accusations of sexual assault in one week. That was Barbara's limit. She no longer cared to maintain a façade of a marriage, or to work with him to manage his humiliations over the disgusting sex tape which she saw as a sort of divine retribution for his sins, and Barbara just knew the allegations against her husband were true. In all of their preparation for their joint statement about the sex tape, Walter never mentioned his assault was triggered by his sexual misconduct.

Walter received a phone call that was very unwelcome, but he didn't have the option of not taking it.

"Walter, we need to talk."

Words Walter didn't want to hear at this moment, especially from the head of the media group of which Overlord Productions was a part, a rather minor part. He'd been at the helm of Overlord for the past fourteen years, the chief executive officer of the powerful film company, but he wasn't the owner. He served at the will of the board of directors, a mostly ornamental group of wealthy businessmen convening yearly, usually to rubber-stamp whatever policies were written by the men and women who actually ran the company.

The six members of the board of directors for Overlord Productions were appointed by the CEO of the huge media group with whom Walter was now speaking. Walter often said the board of directors were the highest paid people in all of Hollywood if you did the math on their yearly stipends and how much time they actually worked. It turned out to be somewhere around eighty thousand dollars for a morning's work.

"Sure, when can we meet?" Walter asked his media group overlord.

"We're talking now. This is extremely time sensitive."

Walter knew this was not going to be a good phone call.

"We need you to resign immediately as CEO of Overlord," his boss, Joseph Hall said. "Christ, Walter, you must know this better than anyone."

Walter's famous temper was flaring.

"Resign? I fucking built this company, I'm sure I don't have to remind you of that. I can't believe..."

He was cut off.

"Walter, this isn't a request. You fight this and you'll leave with nothing. Read your contract. Resign quietly, and you'll be well taken care of, but it has to be today. Now."

Read your contract. As if anyone but a lawyer had ever read one of those fifty-page treatises where clarity goes to die.

Walter knew how things worked at this level of corporate America well enough to realize that hanging on to his position would be a difficult matter in the face of his current legal problems, even if he had the backing of the president of Imperium Media Group. He knew the lawyers would try to take him down, urged on like hounds in a fox hunt. He suddenly felt pure hatred for lawyers, as if they were solely responsible for his current situation shaping up to be an epic downfall. Not for a moment did he think his own actions were responsible for his fall from grace, such is the mind of a sociopath.

"Fourteen years I've been running this film company and this asshole tried to fire me over the phone!" Walter said to his second in command at Overlord. "Hall thinks he can jerk the board of directors around like marionettes, which he could if Overlord wasn't one of the most profitable production companies in this fucking town."

Walter's vice president wasn't nearly as confident as his immediate boss on this matter. On the other hand, he had no illusions of taking Walter's job when the ax fell. If the parent company was going to take out the trash, they'd take it all out at once, which meant the entire executive body. They'd start from scratch to wash away all of the sins of Walter Greene and his VP knew as soon as he heard about Walter's legal problems that his destiny was tied directly to his current boss.

The VP figured the parent company would provide Walter with a proverbial golden parachute if he bowed out gracefully. That didn't mean he, too, would be compensated at the same level as the first in line, so if Walter wanted to stand up and fight, he'd stand behind him, at least until he could find another position. His loyalty to Walter was probably equal to Walter's loyalty in his direction, the VP thought. It was all about money at this level.

Walter was equally recalcitrant toward the criminal prosecutions building up around him. He flatly denied any and all allegations of rape and sexual misconduct, insisting his relations with his female accusers were consensual. He was escorted to Los Angeles Police Department headquarters by two of his lawyers, where he was placed under arrest for the rape of Marjorie Wallace who was a production assistant on an Overlord TV series. He was booked and released under a five-million-dollar bail agreement. He was also forced to surrender his passport and made to wear an ankle monitor with the understanding he wouldn't leave the greater Los Angeles area.

This was the first of what would be nine charges brought against the film magnate. Walter denied all allegations against him and vowed to fight them all in court.
And then Greene's wife filed for divorce.

CHAPTER SEVENTEEN

He wished he could say Los Angeles was starting to grow on him, but Tag despised the city even more with every passing month. He was definitely in a gilded cage, though he'd found a place in Manhattan Beach where he could at least pretend his world didn't revolve around driving. He was grateful he didn't need to get in his car for his day-to-day errands and only ventured out of his ocean-view enclave to work.

How could he leave the City of Angels when he had so much going on? It was full of super-rich assholes with much bigger problems than their economic inferiors. If you interviewed one hundred rich creeps, Tag figured about ninety-eight of them could use the sort of services he offered, and the remaining two wanted things he refused to do.

He was no one's idea of a saint, and there were things he wouldn't do for money, but the things not on his menu could be counted on one hand.

"You want me to cut down a tree and the client gives me fifty thousand cash?" Tag asked on the secure messenger service.

Tag was dealing again with the law firm of Bishop and Sharp of Torrance, California, contracted by Strauss, Merkle, & Randolf. The Beverly Hills firm was represented again by Marty Evans, who'd yet to show up at the lavish strip mall offices of Roland Bishop. In fact, Marty arrived forty-five minutes early and was sitting a few stores away from the law offices, surveilling the lot for any trace that the law offices were being surveilled by someone else.

Ten minutes before the scheduled time of the appointment with Bishop, Marty saw Tag drive around the lot slowly. Tag spotted Marty in his car and parked next to him.

"Waiting for me?" Tag said.

"Don't mind me, just a paranoid ex-cop."

The two walked up to the front door of the law offices and rang the buzzer.

"Marty, you remember Tag," Bishop said with the slightest trepidation in his voice, not completely convinced that Marty hadn't told Tag about his run-in with Morgan.

The three men walked to Bishop's sumptuous office in the back.

"I've been briefed on my latest contract. I just need to know if I'm supposed to be at the top of this tree to collect the fifty thousand. What the fuck? The guy never heard of a tree service?"

Marty laughed at this.

"Nothing like that. The tree's on his neighbor's estate, and it's blocking his view."

"Jesus, fucking rich people," was all Tag could say.

The meeting concluded. Marty hadn't even bothered to sit down.

"Let's take a drive, Tag," he said. "Roland, see you next time."

Tag followed Marty out of Torrance toward the beaches, stopping at a bar where they'd done business in the past. Beers for both men.

"So, you OK with the tree trimming job?"

"If nothing else, it'll make a great story," Tag said, and a story he could tell normal citizens without horrifying them too much. "Can't believe you even showed up for this silly errand."

Marty took a pull from his beer.

"Something else I wanted to pass on to you, concerning the work you did for us a few months ago."

Tag had no idea the actor had almost been killed in a hit and run incident, nor had he been aware the video he made went public, very public.

"Jesus, Tag. You never read a newspaper, watch TV, or go on the internet?" Marty asked. "It's only been national news the past two weeks or so."

"Been busy."

Marty passed his phone across the table with the photo of Morgan.

"This guy was probably responsible for the attempted murder of Pilar Domingo, and he killed Carrie Gold, the actress."

"Never heard of either of them. Should I?" Tag asked.

Marty didn't think that information was required knowledge for every adult, but he had to wonder what other gaps Tag had in his knowledge of popular culture. He was living in Los Angeles, after all. It would be like living in Washington D.C. and not knowing the name of the president.

"Doesn't matter. What does is Gold and Domingo were targeted because of Greene. He contracted someone to hunt down whoever was responsible," Marty said, then pointed again at his phone. "That's him. I'd imagine that…"

"He's coming for me."

Marty nodded.

"What's that mean, exactly? He's coming for the person who did it, or he's coming for me? What does he know?" Tag asked.

"Jack shit, to be honest. He may have a description of you, we're not sure."

Tag pressed Marty on this issue, but Marty had been on the other end of countless interrogations and wasn't about to give in, to say anything to Tag about Bishop and his big mouth, figuring Tag would kill Bishop simply on principle. He scheduled the meeting at Bishop's office simply to deflect suspicion away from the lawyer, assuming Tag would think Marty would never have him cross paths with the guy who'd sold him out.

This explained why Marty staked out the law office beforehand. It would've been a wild coincidence, but Morgan might have been staking out the place that very day. Marty was a careful man, and he'd been a victim of crazier coincidences.

"No more work for you in Los Angeles, if you'd accept any advice from me," Marty said.

"Can I still do the tree job?" Tag laughed.

"Yeah, the cash is up front, I demanded that," Marty said, putting a small package of cookies on the table containing five hundred one-hundred-dollar bills—handing money over in brown paper bags was about as obvious as hiring a skywriter to announce a payoff.

Tag took the cookies and put them in his bag.

"One more thing, another job for you, sort of related to what I told you before."

Tag feigned irritation.

"I'm thinking of retiring, Marty."

"Don't be an asshole. What would you do if you retired?"

"Go to music school," Tag said without a moment's hesitation.

"What? You're a musician?" Marty asked, almost dumbfounded.

Tag waved his outstretched hand back and forth slightly in the universal signal for "so-so."

"Jazz piano, just a hobby, but I've been at it a long time. Self-taught, the two worst words in a musician's vocabulary."

"I'm impressed," Marty said, and he truly was. "See, I got nothing to fall back on. I'll be at this, whatever the fuck I'm doing, until I drop dead."

"I've never met a retired cop who was anything more than a falling-down drunk, and never met a retired criminal of any sort. I hope to be a first," Tag said.

"Well, before you run off to Juilliard or Berklee, I have something for you that pays a lot more than improving the view for some rich prick."

Tag sat back and took a long drink of his beer.

"And how do I know I won't get sold out again like before?"

"Because the guy who's hunting you down is the piece we need taken off the board."

***

The conference room at Barrens & Huntley was more impressive than anything Walter Greene had at his disposal at Overlord Productions, but while the law firm needed to wow outsiders and instill within them the power and magnificence of their work, the deals at the film studio mostly happened behind the scenes and people outside the company were the ones trying to impress the masters at Overlord. Walter realized this, yet he was still comforted by the show of force around him at the table.

Charles Huntley headed up the team from his firm even though his area wasn't criminal law; two other members would represent Greene at the coming trial. Huntley was there as a show of respect for one of the firm's top clients in his time of need. Along with Huntley and the two criminal trial specialists, there were three investigators, two lawyers aiding the defense team, and two paralegals. This was one of the biggest criminal cases the firm had represented, and Charles Huntley wanted to overwhelm the prosecution before the case even went to trial.

Everyone was at their battle stations when Walter took a seat at the table. The lead defense lawyer began.

"The D.A. is fucking up completely, in my opinion, by beginning with the Daniels case. They think they're putting their best foot forward because it's a felony rape charge, but their case is weak. No DNA evidence, the accuser never reported the incident to authorities, they have no corroboration, it's basically her word against ours. On top of that, the D.A. is desperately trying to get us to take a deal which would be nothing more than a fine."

"And you don't want to take it?" Huntley asked, just for Walter's sake as he knew the answer.

"Would you if you were positive you were going to win? Maybe if this were all they were going to throw at Mr. Greene, I could see it, but we need to destroy their case to make subsequent charges look equally meritless."

"What will be the next salvo from the D.A., if you had to venture a guess?" Huntley asked, mostly for Walter's benefit.

"We think it'll be the Margoli case, simply because it's generated the most press, but it's also a weak case with zero evidence."

"And what about the accusations made by Pilar Domingo? Will this make it to court?" Huntley asked, genuinely looking for an answer.

"Unless her condition improves enough for her to take the stand, I doubt it."

"What do we know?"

One of the investigators took this question.

"She's more or less in a coma and critical condition. Still in the same hospital in Valencia, Spain, where she was admitted, not a good sign and she has no family there and would've presumably been transferred if she were physically able," the investigator said. "She may never be able to speak again, let alone serve as a witness."

"Her testimony she gave to her law firm before the accident is troublesome," the defense lead lawyer admitted. "The prosecution may not need anything else from her."

Walter hadn't said a word up to this point.

"What an ungrateful cunt," he finally exploded.

Even with no women present, everyone in the room winced, everyone except Walter.

"I did so much for her, and then she comes out with this fairy tale."

Walter Greene's legal team would never allow him to say a single word if they ever went to trial, knowing this sort of outburst wouldn't sit well with a jury, but Huntley understood the value of having a defendant so convinced of his innocence, even if he were a compulsive liar. It was agreed there'd be no deals made with the D.A.'s office. They'd attack each accusation and try to keep it from ever coming to trial while being confident of winning any case the prosecution could throw at them.

Walter had let Morgan know he wanted revenge at any cost. The only loose ends in the matter were the two men who made the video. Months later, Walter demanded a meeting.

They met in the same parking lot. This time, Morgan was early and in the exact spot when Walter had waited for him. Once again, they drove away in Morgan's vehicle.

"It would've been easier, legally, if you'd killed the bitch, but this is even better in a lot of ways. The hit and run thing was brilliant," Walter said.

Morgan drove without responding. He was waiting for a question.

"What about the two sick bastards who did it?"

"I tracked one of them down through some half-assed law office in Torrance Domingo's Beverly Hills firm uses for its dirty work. He's the big guy. I was able to identify him from the video from the tattoos they tried to hide, guy named Victor Martínez, thirty-four years old."

"So, what's the problem? Can't locate him?"

"He's in LA county lock-up awaiting trial on a possession charge."

"Can't you get at him inside? Or bail him out."

"Impossible to bail him out anonymously. I could go through a bail bondsman, but I'd still need a patsy to sign for it. Getting at him in lock-up is actually easier but costly."

"I paid you to get the job done. Quite a lot, in case you've forgotten," Walter said, his anger rising.

"Exactly, you paid me to take care of him. I can't do that if he's inside meaning I have to contract out for someone else to do it. I'm making progress, but it ain't gonna be cheap."

"Christ, you're as bad as my lawyers."

Walter was a little shocked by Morgan's poor grammar, thinking he was some sort of sophisticate from the little contact they had before. Who the hell still said "ain't" without being ironic these days?

"Who can you get to do it and how much is it going to cost?" he asked.

"Some Compton gang thugs. They're jerking me around some. If I were some nigger, they'd probably do it for five hundred bucks."

Walter couldn't help but wince, shocked by Morgan's racism, wondering how he felt about Jews before concluding that eloquence and an open mind weren't requirements for a hitman. How some ill-educated White supremacist was going to deal with a Black street gang was something Walter didn't need to know, but he agreed to pay whatever it took, within reason.

There were probably even worse neighborhoods in LA than this corner of Compton off of Alameda, Morgan thought as he

218

approached the address he was given, but it would be difficult to find anywhere outside of a toxic waste dump with less charm. It made Torrance seem like a vacation destination. He parked his car in the street in front of the house wondering if it'd be there when he concluded his business inside.

Once again, Morgan's link to this miserable corner of the city came from a law office he worked with on occasion, further proof lawyers would do anything, work with anyone, and break any existing law for the right price, but he knew he was no one to judge.

There was a kid sitting on the rail of the area too small to serve as a porch, baggy trousers, white T, and a bored look on his face. He didn't say a word or even look in his direction when Morgan walked by and rang the bell.

The iron security gate door would have been a formidable barrier in a police raid and took a good thirty seconds of wrangling with bars and a lock to open before Morgan was escorted into the empty kitchen and told to take a seat at the table.

He sat.

Three very tall young men walked into the kitchen with what Morgan thought were limps, like when people have one limb longer than the other, but they were clad in athletic wear and looked like professional athletes. Morgan was dressed in a blue blazer and chinos with the idea of impressing the gang with his elevated status. They didn't appear impressed in any way.

One of them sat at the table, the other two loomed over it, staring off in opposite directions as if they were on a mountain peak with a 360-degree panorama.

"Let's get to it," the thug at the table said.

No introductions, no names, no greetings.

"I need a guy in LA county lock-up taken out," Morgan said, sounding more relaxed than he felt.

"I heard that part already. We get fifty K for that kind of deal."

That was a starting point, like haggling at the market in Marrakech, not that Morgan had been to Morocco.

"This isn't the president of the United States I'm asking you to kill. He's some nobody scumbag. The police won't even give a shit, just one less case to process, one less total loser in prison."

They negotiated a price, then the gang leader tried to jack up Morgan for the full amount up front, a move he was prepared for as he came with nothing in cash.

"You get the retainer thirty minutes after I leave, the rest when it's a done deal," Morgan said. "Two guys on a motorcycle will roll up out front. Are we cool?"

His negotiating partner at the table didn't feel words were necessary and simply nodded, then swung his head slowly toward the door communicating to Morgan to get out of his house.

Morgan's car was there when he walked out.

Twenty-five minutes later, a GP Moto bike with two men on it came to a stop in front of the house in Compton, the passenger pulled out a canvas pouch and tossed it to one of the two men standing on the sidewalk, then the bike tore away as if it were leaving the pit area and getting back in the race.

Two days later Victor Martínez was beaten to death in the LA county lock-up. There were no witnesses. His life had cost Morgan ten thousand dollars, but he came out twenty grand ahead because he charged Greene three times that amount.

Now Morgan just had one last detail to clear up. He also had other things on his mind lately.

What do you dream about when you're the cause of so many nightmares? Morgan hated sleeping. Going to bed, no matter how exhausted, was unpleasant. He looked upon it as nothing more than a necessary evil. He'd rather dig a grave than sleep, if given the choice.

Morgan had dug a grave or two over the course of his career, deciding early on burial was more discreet than leaving a body in the trunk of a car, as he'd done with his first victim, his molester, although that crime had never come back on him.

Besides sleeping, he could think of a lot of other tasks worse than digging a grave. Just off the top of his head, washing dishes was a lot less gratifying. Dishes just got dirty again, but he was never obliged to dig the same grave twice. Like some kind of curse, he had to sleep every day.

When asked, he said he never remembered his dreams. He never spoke about them and hated more than anything to listen to other people recount their silly subconscious or unconscious short-circuiting, which was Morgan's opinion of this phenomenon. While he felt dreams had no meaning, he couldn't understand why he had so many about his impoverished childhood, particularly of one squalid apartment where he and his mother lived with another woman and her two children back when he was a child.

The dream, the nightmare, was recurring, and varied little: he was alone, trapped in the filthy apartment with the windows boarded and the door nailed shut while he ran out of air. The poverty depicted in the nightmare was more disturbing to him than suffocating. He was asthmatic as a child and knew the horrors of being unable to take in a sufficient amount of air, but being poor was by far his greatest fear. It wasn't even the poverty that tormented him in this nightmare, but the shame he'd felt being poor.

He'd been affluent far longer now than he'd been poverty-stricken, so why couldn't his dream reflect his better times?

What he thought was even stranger was he never dreamed about some of the darker things he did to earn everything he had now. It was like he was being punished for his childhood, a period of his life over which he had no control. He often wondered what it'd be like if the nightmares that haunted him revealed aspects of the sordid work he did instead of his neglected upbringing. Would his sleep be less tortuous?

Alcohol didn't help much, but it beat the shit out of being sober. Did everyone who drank too much suffer from frightful dreams? Morgan hated drug addicts, even smokers. He saw them as weak individuals unable to resist temptations destroying their lives. He never saw his heavy drinking in the same light. To him, it was a kind of medicine, something he managed carefully and never let affect his work. But no matter how much he drank, too often he woke in a cold sweat, gripped by feverish dreams of living in that filthy apartment with his mother.

CHAPTER EIGHTEEN

Morgan had to dig deep to find any public mention of the death of Victor Martínez; a jailhouse execution of a career criminal wasn't much of a news item. Morgan wasn't joking when he told the Compton gang no one cared about the big guy. California's prison homicide rate was more than double the national, hinting that the state didn't care much about anyone behind bars.

Through one of his police contacts, Morgan got shirtless photos of Martínez from one of his rounds through the California penal system, illustrating his many tattoos. He showed them to Walter.

"Maybe," said Walter.

Morgan compared the tattoos from the police photos to video stills from the sex tape, pointing out how the intruders had tried to disguise the prison ink with bigger, phony tattoos painted over the real artwork.

"He's the same size and weight as our target, at least at the time of his death. He looks a lot thinner in these older mug shots and body prints from five years ago."

Greene needed more convincing.

"He bragged about the video to his cellmate. Got that first-hand."

Morgan felt Martínez was his man and had no trouble telling a little white lie to strengthen his case.

"So, we got only two things to clear up. The first question is do you want to make it public that this Martínez pig was the guy from the video? I could leak it out."

Walter hadn't thought about this.

"I don't see how it could possibly incriminate you. Creeps get beaten to death all the time in lockup," Morgan said. "There were more than thirty prison murders last year alone."

The idea of letting the world know the man who raped him had died a horrible death in prison had considerable appeal for Walter.

"Let me think about it but get everything in motion if that's my decision. I want to know exactly how you'll go about making it public."

Morgan nodded and continued.

"OK, now we just have the matter of the guy with the camera, obviously the brains, as this Martínez was a fucking half-wit, at least from the looks of his arrests which include everything from petty shoplifting to public urination. The other guy might be a retard, too. Hard to say."

"What do you have so far?" Walter asked.

"Plenty. It shouldn't be more than a week, two tops."

This was no little white lie; this was full-blown bullshit. Morgan had next-to-nothing on the man he was hunting other than the vague description given by the lawyer.

"This time it'll be very low-key, like a car accident or falling down a flight of stairs so it ain't never coming back on you."

It ain't never coming back on you? This grammatical war crime came as a slap in the face to the Harvard magna cum laude graduate Walter Greene. Walter couldn't decide if he was being

224

an asshole grammar Nazi or if he'd erred in hiring such a syntactically-challenged hitman. He thought it wiser not to correct the hired assassin.

Morgan delivered on two out of three of his targets, and he'd done it in spectacular fashion. He had no qualms about faking this last job, collecting his full fee, and disappearing from the city. He just needed the perfect set of circumstances for the fate he was planning for the videographer in Greene's sex tape.

He'd narrowed it down to one of two choices. He could either find a recent death in the area whose identity could plausibly be the man he was after, or he could kill someone who fit those characteristics. While he searched for a likely victim, he perused every newspaper in the LA area for a death that would match his needs. In whatever way he resolved the matter, Morgan was determined to be on his way in two weeks. Greene had never seen the man and could never identify him, except perhaps from his voice, and that was doubtful. Greene may never hear his voice again if things went as planned for Morgan.

***

Marty Evans read about Victor Martínez's death a day after it happened. Some habits of an ex-cop never die, and one of them for Marty was uncovering news about prison deaths in California. When you've sent as many men to prison as a career LA detective, you like to know who out there is alive or dead, because the dead can't come back to haunt you; convicts with a grudge definitely can.

It was entirely possible Victor Martínez had simply pissed off the wrong person on the wrong day, but, once again, Marty didn't believe in coincidences. If it wasn't a coincidence, it meant

Morgan was probably still in Los Angeles cleaning up for Walter Greene.

While Morgan had given up his hunt for the man behind the break-in at the mansion and now was simply looking for a patsy to collect his fee, Tag was getting paid a lot of money to find Morgan. A man with Walter Greene's business acumen would call it being "incentivized." Pilar Domingo's revenge fund had allotted a fortune to finance an operation if Walter Greene struck back against her. Tag was going to be paid more for this next round of violence than for his initial attack against the Hollywood producer.

Tag had done too many heinous acts for hire to judge anyone else, but he hated men who harmed women or children. Once again, based on the things he'd done for money, he knew he couldn't feel any sort of moral superiority over fixers with absolutely no compunction in doing anything for a paycheck, and although he'd never killed a woman, he was capable of understanding scenarios in which this wasn't unthinkable.

One scenario was a man in Walter Greene's position who had a woman pay two thugs to rape him while making a video of the crime. That man might be justified in striking back at her, even murdering her. Of course, that fictional scenario didn't include the mitigating circumstances, as lawyers were so fond of saying. Walter Greene assaulted Pilar Domingo and many other women and used his position of immense power in the film industry to keep his victims silent. Greene got off lucky with his non-consensual sex tape. All of this Tag rolled around in his head.

Now Tag was being paid a fortune to hunt down the man who killed Pilar Domingo or at least came desperately close to murdering the actor. Tag had no problem accepting this follow-up assignment, because, well, work was work.

Maybe the motherfucker had it coming, Tag thought, but he wondered why Marty Evans was putting so much on finding the hitman Greene hired while letting Greene walk away from all of it.

"He's not walking away from anything," Marty said.

Most of the time, Tag and Marty communicated via a couple of cheap mobile phones, not exactly the most secure system, but adequate for their needs. Today was face-to-face, in a bar off Wilshire and La Ciénaga Boulevard.

"Greene and this Morgan must be pretty chummy these days. If we could track Greene, I'm guessing we could catch the two of them together," Tag said.

Marty had the same thought, but he also knew it was a long shot, to put it mildly. It would require putting a device on Greene's car, or cars, and then being close enough to move in if it seemed he was meeting with his hitman. The only solution in the vast expanse of Los Angeles, which spans hundreds of square kilometers, was electronic tracking.

"But that's some CIA caliber hijinks," Tag said, as if finishing Marty's thoughts on that level of sophistication. "Just tailing someone out here in this traffic is a nightmare, but I'm not telling you anything new."

"Tailing someone is impossible without a helicopter. LAPD's working on drones, but there are still a lot of things to work out with the technology."

Tag had nothing to add to this, but something was bugging him.

"Ever thought about just ending this?"

"How so?" Marty asked.

"I don't know. Just seems this whole 'an eye for an eye' thing has left a lot of blind people, and more to come," Tag said. "I realize this goes against my own interests, but just thought I'd throw that out there."

Marty was blinded by the vicious assault on Pilar Domingo, a woman he barely knew but had come to admire and respect. He only wished he could have talked her out of her assault on Greene.

"She was right, you know," Tag said.

"What?"

"The actress, Domingo. She was right. That prick has already beaten one rape charge against him, or it looks like he will. He'll probably get the other charges thrown out, too," Tag said. "The wonders of having the best legal advice available."

"Fucking LA prosecutors couldn't find their own pricks with both hands," Marty spat out. "Exhibit A: OJ walked. A slam-dunk and he walked."

"Money walks? Is that where that expression comes from?"

"Not positive, but I think it's older than the OJ trial," Marty said. "And I think you have it backward. It goes, 'Money talks, and bullshit walks.' But maybe there's another one."

"That's it," Tag said.

He looked at Marty.

"I forgot what we were talking about."

"Maybe abandon our crusade against Greene? I tried to talk Pilar out of this whole thing from the beginning. After Mr. Hollywood Rapist side-stepped the first charges against him, I realized she had the right idea…"

"Except we should have killed the pig that first time," Tag said, finishing Marty's thought.

"That's exactly what I told her. I also told her Greene would come after her."

"Would Greene be stupid enough, brazen enough to make another attempt against her?" Tag asked.

"He's a serial rapist. Who knows what he's capable of?" Marty asked.

"Murder, as we've already seen," Tag said.

"So, still think we should turn the other cheek?" Marty asked.

"Never said that. Not a big 'turn the other cheek' guy for obvious reasons relating to my profession," Tag said. "I just made a suggestion, but, yeah, this Greene needs to meet his maker, and *pronto*, as we say in Spanish."

"Let's make that happen, along with this Morgan asshole."

"Greene's a public figure, but Morgan's a ghost, like me. I wouldn't envy anyone trying to hunt me down. I'm sure he's trying."

"We know he's trying. He found Pilar and Victor. What makes you think he can't track you down?" Marty asked.

"Tracking me down is one thing, taking me out will present another completely different set of problems for Mr. Morgan," Tag said. "And by the way, if I end up dying in a car crash out here, don't automatically give credit to him. Every time I get out of my car alive it seems like some sort of miracle I survived. I felt safer in Iraq than on the San Diego Freeway."

"Greene has security so far up his ass after the break-in they probably shower with him," Marty said. "He'll be a hard target."

"You just need better intel on the guy," Tag said.

"That's always a plus."

"I'd wager every single woman who works anywhere near the guy would be your ally in this, if you can figure out how to reach them."

Marty hadn't considered this but immediately saw how obvious this was, while forming a risk-free strategy to approach women in Walter Greene's inner circle.

From Pilar Domingo's deposition to her lawyers at the law firm of Strauss, Merkle, & Randolf, Marty had the names of over a dozen women she testified were victims of Greene's abuse. Four of them were currently working at Overlord Productions in various capacities from secretarial to production assistance. While they were all unwilling to risk their jobs by filing complaints against their boss, Marty thought it wouldn't take much prodding for them to sell him out if they could do it anonymously.

He just needed a way to approach these potential allies, pitch his plan, and keep his identity from them so as not to implicate his employers at Strauss, Merkle, & Randolf whom he feared more than the LAPD or the Los Angeles District Attorney's Office. He was thinking out loud and Tag offered an idea.

"Have them contact you like we communicate, or how we did before we became partners or whatever the hell we are these days," Tag said.

Marty made only one phone call, choosing a woman who'd suffered a lot by Greene's actions, according to the statement made by Pilar to her lawyers. It didn't take much for him to convince the woman in Greene's administrative staff to cooperate with him.

"I'm an independent investigator looking into Greene's sexual assaults and his possible involvement in the attack on Pilar Domingo," Marty said to Cynthia Albright.

"I've heard about that, but Greene says it's a lie," she said.

She took a moment to think this over.

"But, of course, he'd say that. He denies all of the rape allegations."

"I need your help," Marty said.

"I'd never speak out against him. Look how he's already having cases tossed out right and left. I need this job."

"I'm not asking you to testify or file a complaint; I need you to be my eyes and ears inside his office."

"I'd lose my job, for starters."

"I'll lose my job if anyone but the two of us find out about this," Marty said, not knowing if this would comfort or further terrify the young woman.

Her end of the phone was quiet.

"Don't you want him to pay for his crimes? You can do that without your name coming up. I swear."

Cynthia Albright was terrified of the idea, but Marty explained how their method of communication would be completely anonymous and impossible to trace back to her. She'd also be paid $50,000 in cash for her efforts.

"When do I start?"

"Now."

Cynthia said she had access to Walter's daily schedule as his moves needed to be coordinated with various divisions at Overlord. Cynthia worked with the finance department. Greene's personal assistant kept his calendar and scheduled almost all of the CEO's appointments. There were often gaps in Greene's day his PA didn't share with everyone, but for the most part, his daily routine was no great secret.

Marty told the secretary to only communicate via their shared drop box when she had access to an outside internet connection. She used the Wi-Fi in one of four nearby coffee shops to send and receive messages. Cynthia was comforted by Marty's somewhat paranoid system. He'd purposely gone a little overboard on security to assuage any fears she might have about betraying her boss, knowing the extreme lengths she had to take would boost her confidence.

The first thing he learned was Greene never went anywhere without a driver and a bodyguard. Marty guessed the driver, too, was a trained security expert. The driver would wait in the car during most appointments while the bodyguard cooled his heels in a lobby or waiting room when Greene was in a meeting or doing whatever it was he did during his working hours. When the CEO went to a restaurant for lunch or dinner, both the bodyguard and the driver waited in the car. At least this was the routine Marty could patch together after a couple of days of surveillance and the intel he got from Cynthia.

CHAPTER NINETEEN

On an average day, somewhere in the neighborhood of 160 people die in Los Angeles County, including thirty-two from coronary heart disease, nine from stroke, and nine from injuries (homicide, suicide, and unintentional). For his purposes, an unintentional death was the best candidate, so of these nine daily accidental deaths, perhaps two or three were worth investigating.

Morgan was looking for a white male between thirty and fifty-five years old who'd died in an accident of some sort. Single or divorced would be more convincing for the fiction he was trying to pass off on Walter Greene about the man who'd broken into his mansion and filmed his rape by Victor Martínez.

The ideal candidate would have a shady work record; a pillar of the community wouldn't serve in the role of a career criminal type hired to commit a felony. Really, anyone who had anything less than a professional career could work. A house painter, a handyman, even a gardener could be a possible front for a hitman or hired thug. For several years, Morgan filed taxes as a tree trimmer to launder part of his illicit income until he learned how to do this more effectively as a real estate broker.

After four days of poring over newspaper and internet searches, he had two prospects for his patsy in the Walter Greene intrusion, although they were both weak. One was a forty-eight-year-old carpenter who fell from a scaffold on a house he was repairing in Culver City. The other younger man died in a traffic accident with no profession given in the news report. Morgan searched the victim's identity online and came up with almost nothing at all.

No online profile was perfect for his needs, and he'd almost made his decision when he read about a man in Orange County who'd been crushed to death under a car he was repairing in his garage. Thirty-four years old, single, never married, and an electronics salesman. Marcus Nelson had no social media accounts Morgan could find. The name was common enough to make a great alias. In fact, it sounded like an alias. His home in Laguna Hills was expensive but not overly extravagant. It could even be described as discreet considering the wealthy zip code.

Morgan had no way to obtain the police report on the accident as Orange County may as well have been Belgium as far as his contacts in the LA area were concerned, but from the news report, it was a freak accident. Marcus Nelson was an experienced automobile hobbyist with a garage full of professional equipment and tools, and his jack failed while he was replacing a muffler on his vintage 1960 El Camino. Morgan knew Greene would appreciate his embellishment on what transpired in Nelson's garage. Greene insisted on hearing the news in person. They met in the same parking lot where they'd spoken on several earlier occasions.

"It's done. I found him a week ago through one of Victor Martínez's old contacts," Morgan said, sitting in the passenger seat of Greene's sedan.

"Done?"

"Dead. Crushed by his own car in his garage."

"No shit?" Greene gasped.

"He lives…excuse me, lived in Laguna Hills. I roll into his driveway and he's under his classic car. I kicked the jack and no more Marcus Nelson."

Greene was impressed.

"I didn't stick around to check his pulse or nothin' but no way he made it. I'll check it out tomorrow. May have another vegetable on our hands like the actress. How she doin'?"

The truth was, Walter had no idea as to the health of Pilar Domingo. Even if she made some sort of miraculous recovery, he was satisfied with Morgan's work. He seemed equally pleased with how the last of his tormentors had met his fate—a fiction created by his fixer.

"I'll get back to you with more specifics, just wanted you to know the last of the assholes who assaulted you is off the board."

Morgan was betting Greene wouldn't investigate this garage accident on his own. He was Greene's investigator, after all. Besides, he knew from the press Greene had much bigger problems. Among other pending charges, he was in the middle of the Valentina Margoli rape trial which was into its third week with the prosecution's case coming to an end.

Most of the legal scuttlebutt concerning the case said Greene's attorneys wouldn't bother to present a defense as they savaged the Italian actor when she was on the witness stand. The defense had shown photos of what Margoli was wearing on the day she was allegedly raped by Walter Greene. She had worn exactly what she was given by the wardrobe department of the TV series *La Frontera Saga* which was produced by Overlord Productions. Now the CEO of that company was using this detail to defend himself. The photos of the beautiful actor in a mini-skirt appeared to carry more weight with the jury than her testimony stating she was wearing what she was told to wear.

The defense had other photos of the actor in revealing clothes posing alongside Greene at publicity events for the series. Margoli's sex life was brought out in as much detail as Greene's lawyers could muster while staying somewhat within the bounds of the law but well outside those of good taste and common decency. Like any victim in a rape trial, it was open season on Valentina Margoli. She defended herself well on the stand, but the legal team representing the film producer had done an exceptional job in selecting the jury.

Rape convictions were always difficult for the prosecution for a host of reasons. There were usually no witnesses to the crime, so it came down to the victim's word against that of the accused. Proving the absence of consent beyond a reasonable doubt is difficult, to say the least.

Unless the crime is reported immediately and a medical examination is administered, there is no evidence. What most people—and potential jurors in rape trials—don't understand is if a woman is raped by someone she knows, she's less likely to report it immediately to the police. This is due to many factors, including shock, fear, and shame. If she is attacked by a stranger in an alley, she's more likely to report the crime immediately.

"Under no circumstances do you want to be raped by some filthy rich asshole," Marty explained to Tag.

"What difference does it make?" Tag asked.

"A private legal team arguing against a public prosecutor is like watching the Harlem Globetrotters play the Generals."

Tag had no idea what this reference implied but imagined it a severe mismatch.

"Greene's lawyers are destroying the prosecution, at least from what I've been hearing. No great mystery why women don't report rapes. A rich prick like Greene would have to confess to get a guilty verdict."

Tag thought it, but he wouldn't say it again: they should have killed Greene after making the sex tape. Getting to the film producer now would be a challenge, to put it mildly. The good news for Tag was he wasn't being tasked with going after Greene again.

"Where are you on closing in on your man?" Marty asked him.

What Marty didn't know wouldn't hurt him. This was Tag's general philosophy regarding most people he dealt with.

"I have some leads."

He didn't, but it was the safe thing to say. Taking out Greene would be a lot easier than chasing down the ghost of the man who ran down Pilar Domingo, even if Greene was surrounded now with a team of ex-Mossad operatives. He could definitely get to Greene; getting away with it was much trickier.

Tag thought of himself as a guy who could get things done, and if that thing happened to be ending someone's life, he was cool with it. Now he was being paid to do something he was almost certain would be impossible. Whoever carried out the attack on Pilar Domingo and killed Carrie Gold, then had Victor Martínez executed in LA lock-up was a formidable adversary, to put it mildly. Greene was probably paying his mercenary to hunt down Tag just like Tag was tasked with the same mission. His opposite must have understood the futility of this as well as he did.

The man working for Greene was like Tag's reflection, a twin. A doppelgänger? What if he'd been tasked to do the things the other guy did? Tag certainly would have accepted the job. Hell, he would have worked for both sides at the same time. Tag's code was flexible, so flexible he'd never really called it a code.

Codes were mostly bullshit, things Tag left behind when he was discharged from the military and was no longer obliged to follow their rules. The Uniform Code of Military Justice, or UCMJ, was something Tag found had very little to do with justice. Spite, vengeance, and retribution were more accurate terms to describe military tribunals and other tools they called "non-judicial punishment" which was like the armed forces' answer to a lousy plea bargain deal. Most soldiers under scrutiny accepted "non-judicial punishment" for the exact same reasons criminals accepted plea agreements, even if they were innocent. Why? Because if you lost, you were completely fucked.

But everyone had to have a code, Tag thought. Something in the way of boundaries, like lanes on the highway, or speed limits, or traffic lights, and even no-parking zones. Without them, there was only chaos. When he thought about it in those terms, Tag realized why he hated driving so much: too many rules, just like life in the military. He could never understand how the automobile had become a symbol of freedom in America. Being able to live without a car was his idea of freedom.

Tag was ready to leave LA after letting Marty know that trying to identify the man who ran down Pilar Domingo was hopeless.

"Listen, Marty. I could tell you I could do it, take more of your money..."

"It's not mine," Marty interrupted.

"I could take more of someone's money, but I'm not going to bullshit you. I have about as much chance of finding this guy as a cure for cancer."

"I think they got one of those."

"What?" Tag asked.

"Like chemo and operations, you know, cures, for cancer."

Tag paused just long enough to contain his exasperation.

"Then have those people look for our guy. We aren't going to find him, not if he doesn't want to be found," Tag said. "I gotta get out of this city if you can call it that. I've driven more in these past few months than in my entire life. Never enjoyed a moment of it."

Marty was LA born and raised and didn't know there was anywhere else on the planet that was habitable. The way most Angelenos saw the world, there was only the ocean to the west, and the east, well, people came west. No one went in the other direction, not by choice.

"So, this fuck who almost killed Pilar gets a pass?" Marty asked.

"I don't get paid to give out passes, Marty. I get paid to do things, and if I can't do something, I'm obliged to say that. I'm saying it now."

"All right. I guess there really is honor among thieves," Marty said. "Everyone has to have a code."

"Funny you say that. Just thinking the same thing."

CHAPTER TWENTY

The victory dinner was at a new Spanish restaurant in the Century City Mall. Greene had talked his wife out of her divorce proceedings, asking her to wait at least until after the Valentina Margoli trial, what his legal team thought was the strongest case against their client. However, as shrewd a negotiator as he was, he probably couldn't have convinced his wife to attend the dinner. The truth was she wasn't invited and a man beating a rape conviction wasn't something women would be inclined to celebrate, even his wife.

Walter no longer had any need to keep up the appearances of the happy family man. He'd won. He'd been winning, and his team predicted this streak would continue until there was nothing in front of them. They worked like a thatcher with a razor-sharp scythe cutting down every charge brought against him.

"The other charges will be like batting away flies," Charles Huntley III assured him. "They'll never make it to trial."

Charles Huntley III made apologies for missing the dinner.

Three of the women who'd brought complaints against Greene had reached financial settlements, probably after seeing his legal team dismantle four cases before trial before winning a not-guilty verdict in the Margoli trial. "Face humiliation or get rich" seemed to be the message from the Greene camp to the victims. Along with the financial settlements came iron-clad non-disclosure agreements forbidding the women to ever speak of the alleged events again, not even off-the-record. If anyone heard them talking about Walter Greene, they'd face ruinous lawsuits.

What would winning against Walter Greene look like? How could any woman stand up to someone as powerful and connected as the CEO of Overlord Productions? Even his parent company couldn't make him step down from his position. His victory over the media group to keep his position dominated a press cycle and captured the attention of the nation, or at least Hollywood.

There was no proof, but the rumors about Walter Greene's involvement in the Pilar Domingo assault were now accepted as fact by many followers of the saga.

Azahar, the trendiest bistro in LA, was on the second floor of the mall and featured cuisine from the Valencia area of Spain, famous for rice and oranges, thus the name meaning orange blossom. Walter knew even less about food than he did about movies, but the restaurant was all the rage among the Beverly Hills foodies, whoever they were. Walter didn't have time for such trivialities as food, but he wanted to be where people of his stature were supposed to be.

Walter thought the menu was a pretentious load of crap printed in Spanish with translations below the menu descriptions. Walter had studied French in high school but made zero effort to continue with his studies once they weren't required, and Spanish seemed like the language of gardeners and maids to him. He'd lived in Los Angeles for almost two decades and never thought to learn even a word of Spanish. It was like living in the sea and never learning to swim.

It was a sad turnout for the dinner with only the legal team including the investigators and the paralegals, which the lead lawyer felt would pad out their representation without Charles Huntley, the firm's leading partner, who'd given a weak

242

justification for his absence—a dead relative—which seemed like even a poor excuse for missing a day of high school.

It was Walter, his legal team, and a few loyal hold-outs at Overlord Productions dining at the trendy Azahar.

"I want to thank all of you for demonstrating to the world my innocence and the hollow nature of these attacks against me, all from women whose careers I've made at Overlord Productions, the company I've dedicated my life to for all these years."

The small party of supporters raised their glasses of expensive wine paid for by Walter Greene, along with everything else they ordered that night.

Toward the end of the five-course menu, a stunning waitress knelt beside Walter.

"There's a woman asking for you, Mr. Greene. She's in the lobby near the elevators."

"What's she look like?"

"Very tall, blonde hair, mid-twenties, and she has some sort of accent, I think."

This checked all of Walter's boxes as he thought of a woman he'd met at a company function a few days ago.

He excused himself from the dinner and made his way out of the restaurant to the second-floor lobby.

Marty Evans was ready to call it all off if it looked like there could be a problem. He was mostly concerned about other people outside the restaurant. He saw one of the two elevators stopped on the floor above and the other on the ground floor. Marty stepped back into the fire stairs exit when he saw Walter leaving the restaurant.

Walter walked out of Azahar into an empty lobby except for a beautiful, blonde woman standing next to the elevator in a short skirt only an incredibly fit body could pull off without looking vulgar.

Marty had opened the elevator with a universal key used in case of emergency when there was a malfunction. The woman was standing in front of the open elevator door when Walter approached her.

"Hello, Walter," the woman almost whispered.

Walter stepped up as if to enter the elevator with his latest conquest.

He didn't realize the elevator door opened into a void. Marty stepped out of the fire exit taking only two steps to come up behind Walter.

"This is from Pilar Domingo, Walter," Marty whispered, pushing Walter on the back while taking the phone Walter had in his left hand.

Walter Greene fell into the open shaft, too surprised even to scream.

Marty put his key into the elevator, closing the door, then pressed the call button which sent the elevator down from the floor above. Marty moved back over to the fire exit and walked down the stairs. The woman took the elevator down to the first level and walked out of the mall.

Marty used Walter's phone that was still activated to send a text to his vice president who was at the dinner.

"A friend wants to show me how happy she is for my victory today. Send my thanks and good wishes to everyone at the table."

It was salacious enough and Walter-like so as not to raise the suspicion of his second in command. The vice president read the text aloud and got a few laughs all around.

Marty scrolled furiously through Walter's messages until he found the contact he was looking for. Then he sent another message to his driver who he expected was waiting along with the bodyguard in the parking garage below the mall.

"Leaving with a woman. See you tomorrow."

From previous messages between Greene and his driver, this didn't seem to be a huge detour in their protocol. It really didn't matter too much at this point but keeping Greene's security out of the picture would further cloud his disappearance. The longer Walter went missing without being reported, the more difficult the investigation would prove for police detectives.

Marty had a man on the third floor who'd held the elevator there so whoever stepped into the open door on the floor below would fall to the bottom of the shaft five floors below in the parking garage under the mall.

The video camera on the second floor by the elevators had been obstructed by this same man moments before Walter was called out of the dinner. When he received Marty's signal to release the elevator, he walked down the stairs, removed the obstruction from the video camera, then went down to the basement garage level and reactivated the video surveillance near that elevator. He had also interrupted video cameras in two other elevators to lead police to believe the overall system was flawed and not just the cameras for the elevator where the accident had occurred.

Walter Greene wasn't reported missing until thirty-six hours later, and his body wasn't recovered at the bottom of the elevator shaft until two days after the victory dinner. The waitress who'd relayed the message from the woman in the lobby was never interviewed, a typical breakdown of the LAPD investigation process. The mall security video footage was inconclusive as there'd been several lapses on that level during several days prior to Greene's fatal fall. These video malfunctions were also caused by Marty's accomplice as soon as Greene knew the location of the planned dinner after the trial—forwarded to him by Greene's secretary. Police investigators found the video lapses to be sketchy, but they weren't ready to jump to any conclusions.

There was no sign of foul play, and the unfortunate incident was deemed a freak accident. Walter Greene had simply been the victim of a faulty elevator. He'd probably been sending a text when the door opened to an open shaft—Marty left a partial message on Walter's phone police could only assume was interrupted by his fall, managing to drop his phone on the floor before he fell. He considered sticking around the shopping center and then tossing Greene's phone down the elevator shaft after he sent the messages on it, but it was too risky, lengthening his exposure time at the scene of the crime. The police certainly couldn't prove someone had taken the phone from Greene while he was still alive, and with no other available evidence, it was just as likely someone found the phone on the floor and made off with it.

There was no clear evidence of foul play in the death, and police were loathe to jump to that conclusion. Los Angeles registered over three hundred murders the previous year, they had their hands full with bona fide homicides. Had the deceased been anyone less than a Hollywood film mogul, LAPD would have written it off immediately as an accident.

While it wasn't exactly an "all hands on deck" situation with homicide detectives, they were working the case as a high-profile investigation, but with nothing pointing to murder. There were no firm suspects, although Greene's enemies were nothing short of legion after the trial of the popular, and very outspoken Italian actor. Margoli had an alibi.

After hearing about Greene's fatal drop, Valentina Margoli, the accuser in Greene's rape trial ending in a not-guilty verdict, quickly made public her feelings on the mishap.

"The newspaper said Walter Greene was texting when he stepped into an open elevator shaft. I could name a couple dozen women who'd have gladly given him a push."

The fiery Italian actor, known for not mincing her words, was widely pilloried in the press for her statement, but she refused to apologize, even adding further insult to injury in a nationally televised follow-up interview.

"If Walter wanted people to respect him in death, he should've thought about being a better human being in life."

Few people were willing to go on record saying anything good about Walter Greene. He may have been awarded a not-guilty verdict in the Valentina Margoli case, as well as having five other cases dismissed before trial, but at the time of his death, everyone who still thought Greene was innocent could've shared a single taxi as they were run out of town by the mob.

Greene's position at Overlord Productions was quietly filled by a total outsider from the tech world, a woman. Most of the upper-echelon executives were let go unceremoniously. The deceased CEO had tainted everyone around him who held power at the company. Their loyalty to the former president of the firm had backfired and most of the corporate hierarchy would never find work in Hollywood again. They weren't missed.

EPILOGUE

With the sprawl of Los Angeles and the job behind him, Tag felt a suffocating weight had been lifted off his chest. His stress level went from red-lined to only worrying about what time to light up his cigar in the evenings as he sat on the rooftop terrace of the flat where he was staying in San Miguel de Allende, Mexico.

"I honestly thought I was going to lose it if I had to deal with LA for another second," he said over the phone.

He decided now was as good a time as any to light up his *La Gloria Cubana* Churchill as he looked out over the steeple of the village *iglesia* and a sky with a thin brushstroke of clouds over the mountains.

"Job too much for you, old man?" the voice on the other end asked.

Tag put down his stogie and almost choked on the brandy.

"The job? I'm talking about driving a fucking car, driving a car in LA, to be more precise," Tag countered. "If I never drive a car again, I'll die a happy man."

"You hate driving that damn much? Driving don't bother me."

The bad grammar tic irritated Tag like nails on a chalkboard, but he was no English tutor.

"Especially in that awful place," Tag said.

"Really? I like it here, thinking of staying."

"You gotta be kidding. I wouldn't live there if you paid me by the minute," Tag said. "Aren't things a little hot for you there these days?"

Tag took another good pull on the Dominican cigar.

"Not really. Cops are leaning toward accidental death for Greene. They got nothing else. It ain't never coming back on me," he said on the other end. "Accidental, ha."

Morgan assumed that Walter Greene's accident was Tag's doing, but he wouldn't ask. It just wasn't done among them.

He paused and Tag thought he lost the connection.

"At least he paid me in full before his little mishap," the man added.

If Greene owed him money, then Morgan may have pressed the matter with Tag.

"I'll never tell. The producer was a busy guy. Everyone knows you shouldn't text and walk or drive at the same time," Tag said. "You could step out in traffic or into an open elevator shaft."

"The world's a dangerous place. It don't matter how much money you got."

Again, the man's grammar stopped Tag dead in his tracks, like a spell-check program pausing at an error. He thought about correcting him but stopped. How great does your grammar have to be to do what he does, Tag thought.

"So, what's next for you? Retiring?"

"I don't have any idea of what retiring would look like," Tag said.

"Says the man on a rooftop smoking a cigar."

"Never said I don't take time off. What about you?" Tag asked.

"You ever heard that if you love what you do, you aren't working?"

"I've heard something like that," Tag said, not wanting to correct this fractured aphorism. "But never from anyone in our line of work."

"Probably why I'm better at it than you, Tag."

"You could be right, but work isn't my whole life. As we say in Spanish, I work to live, I don't live to work."

"Of course, they say that. Lazy fuckers."

Stupid and racist was no way to go through life, Tag thought. He also didn't bother explaining Spanish was spoken in over twenty countries on several continents, so just who these "lazy fuckers" were covered a lot of territory.

"How the hell would you know? You've barely been out of the USA," Tag said.

"Why would I leave the greatest country in the world?" he asked, not mentioning his recent trip to Spain.

"You just need to leave the greatest country on earth and find some nice little place without an extradition treaty," Tag said. "Or at least lay low for a while."

Tag could've used some company, but this was no invitation. He doubted the two of them could survive a weekend together. However, he enjoyed their conversations and appreciated his insights. People in his line of work were few and very far between. Was this a friendship? Tag never looked at it this way, but after every talk with Morgan, he felt he learned something about their trade.

"I have to beg your forgiveness, my old friend."

"Why's that?" Tag asked.

"I killed you a while back. Got a good payday out of it, too."

"Please tell me you didn't actually kill someone."

"Naw, man. I just found some random guy got crushed under his car," Morgan said. "I mean, I would've killed someone if this guy hadn't come up."

Tag knew exactly what he was talking about because he'd done the same thing.

"People die every day in the big city, no sense of letting them go to waste," Morgan said. "Remember you telling me that, Tag?"

"Son of a bitch," Tag said, slapping his forehead. "Forgot you learned that little sleight of hand from me. You're welcome, by the way."

Marty offered to pay Tag to track down Morgan and put him in the ground without even insisting on seeing the body, figuring it was in Tag's best interest to hunt down the man who was coming for him. Tag turned down the money. He knew he had nothing to fear from the fixer on the other side of the net.

Tag had used a dead patsy on several occasions for many different reasons, often to patch up holes in his work, or throw off authorities sniffing around after him.

Neither of us will ever have grandchildren, but they'd love some of our stories, Tag thought. But he prayed Morgan would never be a father, which he felt would be like welcoming a new disease into the world.

Tag knew this wasn't how the world worked. Perhaps Walter Greene had perfectly decent parents, yet he turned out to be Walter Greene. Perhaps not. His mother and father could've been almost directly responsible for his criminal behavior. Morgan had confessed the story of his upbringing to Tag which most mental health experts would consider a case of failed parenthood.

Tag gave up a long time ago about judging his failed childhood and almost complete absence of parental supervision. Water under the bridge, *agua pasada* as they said down here. For anything to do with what some would call compromised ethics, Tag blamed his military service where he was paid to commit murder, and then almost went to prison for it, but was simply drummed out of that mercenary corps. From there, he forged a new life of crime, considerably less violent than his former life in the U.S. Army, and much more profitable.

A man has to make his own way, make his own code.

"Pretty slick how you took out the movie guy. Something else you need to teach me," Morgan said.

Tag wasn't sure exactly how Greene had met his maker but wasn't about to set Morgan straight on the matter. He was almost certain that the ex-cop was responsible. Tag also knew that it didn't hurt his reputation if certain people on the inside of their profession thought that not only had he killed a very high-profile target, but that it had been deemed an accident by LAPD investigators.

"Funny how both people who set this all in motion ended up dead," Morgan said.

"What do you mean 'both'?"

"Don't they have TVs down in Mexico?"

"I don't watch TV," Tag said.

"The actress died, too. Couple days ago," Morgan said. "She never came out of the coma."

Feeling one way or the other over the death of a client wasn't part of Tag's code, but this news hit him hard. He'd never even met the actor, but he thought what he did for her served a good cause. Greene deserved it. He also knew that he should've killed the serial abuser after he filmed the rape scene he staged. He actually told the lawyer this and had him communicate this to Pilar Domingo, but she refused. The more Tag learned about Walter Greene, the more he knew there wouldn't be a soul on this earth who would avenge his death and the humiliating rape video. The only person who cared about Walter Greene was himself.

As this was going through Tag's mind, he held the phone away from his ear. He could hear Morgan talking, but he wasn't listening. After a moment, he put the phone to his ear again.

"Listen, man, I have to go. Got someone on the other line, a woman who's coming over."

"Gotcha, talk to you soon…"

Tag ended the call.

The truth was Tag didn't even know what Pilar Domingo looked like, he'd never seen a photo and had never seen her in a film, and as he'd recently admitted, he didn't watch TV. So why was he feeling this, whatever it was? A sense of loss? How was this different from the countless other jobs he carried out in this profession?

In truth, it wasn't any different, yet he felt he was doing something good for the woman. It was similar to how he viewed his first combat tour where he believed he was defending his country. His elation didn't even last through his first firefight in Afghanistan as he realized that "winning" for the U.S. could only come through genocide. No occupying force could ever impose their will on these people.

Lesson learned, he thought. The code doesn't include doing something good—he never saw himself as Robin Hood or Zorro. In fact, most of what he did was the exact opposite of upholding honor or fighting injustice; it meant doing truly awful things, from contract murder to cutting down a majestic coastal cypress tree because it blocked some asshole's ocean view.

His code required him to have the same lack of feeling for a human life as he did for the cypress he felled. He couldn't allow the woman's death to cloud his thoughts. His only concerns were survival and not getting arrested. Once he was paid, and these hurdles cleared, he didn't suffer consequences for his actions.

Consequences were what Tag left in his wake, other people's problems.

www.ingramcontent.com/pod-product-compliance
Lightning Source LLC
Chambersburg PA
CBHW071602180626
46819CB00002B/101